Gene Roddenberry

Star Trek
The Motion Picture

A Novel

Based on the screenplay by Harold Livingston
and the story by Alan Dean Foster

D1337926

Futura Publications Limited

A Futura Book

First published in Great Britain by
Futura Publications Limited in 1979
Reprinted 1980

ISBN 0 7088 1725 4

Printed in Great Britain by
Hazell Watson & Viney Ltd
Aylesbury, Bucks

Futura Publications Limited
110 Warner Road
Camberwell, London SE5

STAR TREK
THE MOTION PICTURE

ADMIRAL KIRK'S
PREFACE

My name is James Tiberius Kirk. *Kirk* because my father and his male forebears followed the old custom of passing along a family identity name. I received *James* because it was both the name of my father's beloved brother as well as that of my mother's first love instructor. *Tiberius*, as I am forever tired of explaining, was the Roman emperor whose life for some unfathomable reason fascinated my grandfather Samuel.

This is not trivial information. For example, the fact that I use an old-fashioned male surname says a lot about both me and the service to which I belong. Although the male surname custom has become rare among humans elsewhere, it remains a fairly common thing among those of us in Starfleet. We are a highly conservative and strongly individualistic group. The old customs die hard with us. We submit ourselves to starship discipline because we know it is made necessary by the realities of deep space exploration. We are proud that each of us has accepted this discipline voluntarily – and doubly proud when neither privation nor physical jeopardy is able to shake our obedience to the oath we have taken.

Some critics have characterized us of Starfleet as 'primitives' and with some justification. In some ways, we do resemble our forebears of a couple of centuries ago more than we do most people today. We are not part of those increasingly large numbers of humans who seem willing to submerge their own identities into the groups to which they belong. I am prepared to accept the possibility that these so-called *new humans* represent a more highly evolved breed, capable of finding rewards in group consciousness that we more primitive individuals will never know.

For the present, however, this new breed of human makes a poor space traveler, and Starfleet must depend on us 'primitives' for deep space exploration. It seems an almost absurd claim that we 'primitives' make better space travelers than the highly evolved, superbly intelligent and adaptable *new humans*. The reason for this paradox is best explained in a Vulcan study of Starfleet's early years during which vessel disappearances, crew defections and mutinies had brought deep space explorations to a near halt.* This once controversial report diagnosed those mysterious losses as being caused directly by the fact that Starfleet's early recruitment standards were dangerously *high*. That is, Starfleet Academy cadets were then being selected from applicants having the highest possible test scores on all categories of intelligence and adaptability. Understandably, it was believed that such qualities would be helpful in dealing with the unusually varied life patterns which starship crews encounter in deep space.

Something of the opposite turned out to be true. The problem was that sooner or later starship crew members must inevitably deal with life forms more evolved and advanced than their own. The result was that these superbly intelligent and flexible minds being sent out by Starfleet could not help but be seduced eventually by the higher philosophies, aspirations and consciousness levels being encountered.

* See STF 7997 B.

8

I have always found it amusing that my Academy class was the first group selected by Starfleet on the basis of somewhat more limited intellectual agility.* It is made doubly amusing, of course, by the fact that our five-year mission was so well documented, due to an ill-conceived notion by Starfleet that the return of the U.S.S. Enterprise merited public notice. Unfortunately, Starfleet's enthusiasm affected even those who chronicled our adventures, and we were all painted somewhat larger than life, especially myself.

Eventually, I found that I had been fictionalized into some sort of 'modern Ulysses' and it has been painful to see my command decisions of those years so widely applauded, whereas the plain facts are that ninety-four of our crew met violent deaths during those years – and many of them would still be alive if I had acted either more quickly or more wisely. Nor have I been as foolishly courageous as depicted. I have never happily invited injury; I have disliked in the extreme every duty circumstance which has required me to risk my life. But there appears to be something in the nature of depicters of popular events which leads them into the habit of exaggeration. As a result, I became determined that if I ever again found myself involved in an affair attracting public attention, I would insist that some way be found to tell the story more accurately.

As some of you will know, I did in fact become involved in such an affair – in fact, an event which threatened the very existence of Earth. Unfortunately, this has again

* EDITOR'S NOTE: We doubt that 'limited intellectual agility' will stand up in the face of the fact that Kirk commanded the U.S.S. Enterprise on its historic five-year mission, becoming the first starship captain in history to bring back both his vessel and his crew relatively intact.

brought me to the attention of those who record such happenings. Accordingly, although there may be many other ways in which this story is told or depicted, I have insisted that it also be set down in a written manuscript which would be subject to my correction and my final approval. This is that manuscript, presented to you here, as an old-style printed book. While I cannot control the other depictions of these events that you may see, hear, and feel, I can promise that every description, idea and word on these pages is the exact and true story of Vejur and Earth as it was seen, heard, and felt by . . .

James T Kirk

AUTHOR'S PREFACE

Considering Admiral James Kirk's comments in his own preface, it may seem strange that he chose me as the one to write this book. I was, after all, somewhat a key figure among those who chronicled his original five-year mission in a way which the Admiral has criticized as inaccurately 'larger than life.'

I suspect that the thing which finally recommended me to the Admiral was the fact that I have always cherished books as much as he does. Or perhaps he thought I would be more trustworthy when working with words rather than with images. Either way, it is clear he knew that he could guarantee the accuracy of this by insisting that the manuscript be read, and, where necessary, corrected by everyone involved in the events being described. Spock, Dr McCoy, Admiral Nogura, Commander Scott, the Enterprise bridge crew and almost everyone else listed on these pages have been given the opportunity to review every word describing the events in which they took any part. These final printed pages reflect their comments as well as Admiral Kirk's determination that this be the whole and full truth of what actually happened in the events described here.

Finally, on a more personal note, why am I concerning myself with the Enterprise and its crew once again? Having depicted them already with at least some popular success, could I not have given this same effort to new and freshly challenging subjects? Of course. Any civilized individual, whether author or not (one is hardly a prerequisite to the other), has no end of events and subjects clamoring for and doubtlessly deserving better attention.

Why STAR TREK again? I suppose the real truth is that I have always looked upon the Enterprise and its crew as my own private view of Earth and humanity in microcosm. If this is not the way we really are, it seems to me most certainly a way we ought to be. During its voyages, the starship Enterprise always carried much more than mere respect and tolerance for other life forms and ideas – it carried the more positive force of *love* for the almost limitless variety within our universe. It is this capacity for *love for all things* which has always seemed to me the first indication that an individual or a race is approaching adulthood.

There may still be long and awkward years for humanity between now and maturity, but we have at last come within some reach of understanding that our future can hold any new dimensions of challenge and happiness that we desire and deserve. While we humans may still be a considerable distance from understanding *truth*, or even of being able to cope with it, I believe that we are at last beginning to understand that *love* is somehow integral to *truth*. Perhaps it demarks the path leading there. Much of my pleasure in Kirk, Spock, McCoy, Uhura, Scotty, Chekov, Chapel and Rand had to do with such thoughts. I have always found some hope for myself in the fact that the Enterprise crew could be so humanly fallible and yet be some of those greater things, too.

CHAPTER ONE

He felt a strange tingling coming from somewhere inside his head. It was as if some intricate mechanical pattern had started to form there. Then that pattern became a memory, and he realized that he was receiving a Starfleet Command alert signal. He did not like the feeling of it – and knowing that it came from a device implanted inside his brain made it even more annoying. As was the custom in Starfleet, indeed it was a requirement, he had been implanted with a senceiver on receiving his first command. It was the ultimate signal device, reserved for use in only the gravest of emergencies – and this was only the second time that Starfleet Command had ever intruded into his mind in this fashion.*

'Is something wrong, Admiral Kirk?'

The question had come from one of the Libyan scholars who traditionally operate the Egyptisraeli Museum at Alexandria. Kirk was on a vacation leave tour of Africa's lovely old cities and had been drawn to the extraordinary history exhibits here in this most famous of all Earth museums. It was, to say the least, an unusual place to receive a Starfleet emergency signal – the surprise of it had brought him halfway to his feet with what he knew

* *EDITOR'S NOTE*: At the time of these events, Starfleet Command's senceiver implants were still being kept secret. Undoubtedly the Admiralty was concerned that the public might mistakenly believe them to be some sort of mind-control device. Clearly, public respect for Starfleet would have been seriously imperiled by anything reminiscent of the horrors that grew out of the politicalizing of behavior control implants and which led to the bloody Mind Control Revolts of 2043–7.

must be a somewhat alarmed look on his face. He managed to shake his head at the Libyan, and then sat down again at the research console he had been using.

It took James Kirk a moment before he could force himself to relax. Actually, he could not have been in a better place in which to receive this kind of emergency message. While pretending to be absorbed in his research console viewer, he could clear his mind of conscious thought and let his implant create images there for as long as the signal lasted.

Then, as the message began to form in Kirk's mind, it started as a powerful kind of daydream. At first a confusion of images, most of them vestiges of his most recent trip, the history studied during this vacation, the museum here, the Libyan scholar. These arranged themselves into patterns which became symbols, faintly familiar alien symbols – then Kirk realized that these symbols were affixed to war vessels.

Klingons!

Kirk found himself seeing three Klingon cruisers which appeared to be moving at warp velocity and in battle formation. The images became more detailed, increasingly real – he could begin thinking about them consciously. The Klingon vessels were big, dangerous looking – undoubtedly their new K't'inga class heavy cruisers which some Admiralty tacticians feared might prove faster and more powerful than Starfleet's First Line Constitution Class starships.

Could that be the point of this alert? Information about an old enemy's new weapon? Kirk immediately discarded that possibility. The existence of a new enemy starship could hardly be classed as an immediately urgent crisis. Nor could this formation of only three Klingon vessels pose any serious threat to Earth or the Federation. This alert must concern something else, something more.

Then with the images firmly established in his mind, Kirk's senceiver implant began to filter the command alert message into his thoughts. As he had guessed, Starfleet had received these images from one of its deep space outposts along the border of the Klingon Empire. This outpost station, Epsilon Nine, had detected the Klingon cruisers in time to get sensor drones launched in time to infiltrate the cruiser formation. Kirk was pleased to see that the Klingons were unaware that they were being shadowed and examined.

The purpose of the drone launch had been to gather intelligence on the new Klingon cruiser design. But once there, the drones had learned something far more important. Something had violated Klingon borders and was passing through their territory and the Klingons were responding in typical fashion. This was heavy cruiser attack formation.

Then the Klingons swept into a wide turn and Kirk could begin to make out an object ahead in that direction. For an instant, he doubted the accuracy of this image he was receiving – it seemed to be merely a *cloud*. True it was strangely luminescent, unlike anything Kirk had ever seen in space before, but why would the Klingons be attacking a cloud? Then, as the cruisers swept closer to it, Kirk began to become aware that the cloud was incredibly large. Then the signal being received by his implant confirmed that it was billions of kilometers in diameter. More, he was made aware that it had passed through Klingon territory so rapidly that this particular cruiser formation had been the only Klingon warships in position to intercept it.

It was all over very fast. The leading Klingon fired a photon torpedo spread toward the heart of the 'cloud'. Its torpedoes simply disappeared – leaving Kirk with the impression that some almost 'godlike' force had simply wished the torpedoes out of existence. Then, as if the Klingons had made something angry, Kirk was aware of a point of green fire emerging from the 'cloud', hurtling toward the cruiser which had fired the photon torpedoes. It was obviously an energy bolt of some sort – then the offending Klingon vessel was enveloped by angry whip-lashes of wild, green energy, crushed, and then it simply imploded into *nothingness*! The other two cruisers were now firing torpedoes too, and were being destroyed as easily and frighteningly.

The 'daydream' ended abruptly. Kirk became aware that the Libyan scholar was again giving him a puzzled look. *Why?* Then Kirk realized what it was. The scholar could see that Kirk was shuddering.

What was his mind suggesting to him? That the Klingons and their vessels had now become wall exhibits in Hell? And where in hell did those words come from? What did they mean?

The 'cloud' thing had merely been passing through Klingon territory, but its interest was not in Klingons or their Empire. It had responded to the attack of their big cruisers with hardly more effort than if it had been brushing away insects. Its interest was elsewhere.

Then Kirk understood what it was that was frightening him. Somewhere in those images received, the command alert had informed him that the frightening huge luminescent 'cloud' was on a precise heading toward a planet named Earth.

CHAPTER TWO

The stonework where Spock knelt was so ancient that its origins could not be traced in even the oldest Vulcan legends. Spock's long robe bore the same patterns as those carved in the ancient stone. The meanings of these symbols were known only to the Vulcan Masters whose abode was here on the high plateau of Gol. Spock had come here not long after the starship Enterprise had completed its historic five-year mission.

It had seemed to Spock that he had no other choice. It was only through the Masters here on Gol that one could achieve *Kolinahr*. And it was only through *Kolinahr* that he could once and for all time unburden himself of his human half which he believed responsible for his pain.

'Spock, son of Sarek of Vulcan and of Amanda of Earth, are thee prepared to open thy mind to us?'

This would be the closest human translation. The words were actually in Old Vulcan and spoken by the Master T'sai. To each side of her stood lesser Masters whose lips moved in an ancient chant in praise of reason.

'I am prepared.'

Spock gave the traditional and expected response. But he was troubled. *Had his answer been the whole truth?* As late as this very morning, he had felt fully prepared to be examined by the Vulcan Masters. During the past nine Vulcan seasons* he had not only survived the disciplines of *Kolinahr*, but also the harsh trials had taken him to those consciousness levels which are beyond the reach of

* In Earth time, 2·8 years.

17

confusion, fatigue and pain. He knew that he had pleased the Masters, even the ones who had at first hesitated over permitting a mere half-Vulcan to become an acolyte in Gol. But no one doubted him any longer – no one but Spock himself.

Until this very morning, Spock had been certain that he had finally and fully exorcised his human half and its shameful emotional legacies. An hour before the rising of the Vulcan suns, Spock had made his way to the high promontory he had chosen as his own and there he had greeted the red dawn of this important day with mind-cleansing meditation. He had known that today he would face T'sai herself and that the High Master would invite him to enter with her into mindmeld so that she might place around his neck the old symbol which proclaimed his mastery of *Kolinahr*. In searching his consciousness this morning, Spock had been especially alert for any trace of pride in his accomplishments here in Gol. *Kaiidth! What was, was!* He had done only what he had been meant to do and had the good fortune to be able to do. With this thought, Spock had looked up at the red dawn sky in the direction where he knew Sol and Earth to be and had begun a respectful, but brief farewell to his mother's planet and the part of his life that it had represented. He had long ago decided that he would neither return to that place nor move among its people ever again.

Jim! Goodbye my . . . my t'hy'la.* This is the last time I will permit myself to think of you or even your name again.

* EDITOR'S NOTE: The human concept of *friend* is most nearly duplicated in Vulcan thought by the term *t'hy'la* which can also mean *brother* and *lover*. Spock's recollection (from which this chapter has drawn) is that it was a most difficult moment for him since he did indeed consider Kirk to have become his brother. However, because

It was at this exact instant that a shockingly powerful consciousness imposed itself unexpectedly into Spock's mind. It was almost as if some powerful *entity* had been searching the galaxy for some long needed answers about Earth and humans and had become aware of Spock's mind at the very instant he was saying his farewell to Earth and Kirk. Although Spock had no idea at the time what it meant, he felt himself being examined almost as if he were a living 'Rosetta stone', capable of understanding both logic and human irrationality, and thus a possible key by which a totally logical entity might understand Earth and humanity.

Most shocking of all, it had frightened Spock. On the morning of the very day that he was to be pronounced free of emotion, he had felt . . . fear. Fear, not so much for himself, but for Earth and for those Earth humans whom he had known for so long and so well.

How was it possible that he felt this? Not only was fear indisputably an emotion, how could he feel that emotion for a planet and a people he had already exorcised from his consciousness and from his life!

'Here on these sands, our forebears cast out their

---

t'hy'la can be used to mean *lover*, and since Kirk's and Spock's friendship was unusually close, this has led to some speculation over whether they had actually indeed become lovers. At our request, Admiral Kirk supplied the following comment on this subject:

'I was never aware of this *lovers* rumor, although I have been told that Spock encountered it several times. Apparently he had always dismissed it with his characteristic lifting of his right eyebrow which usually connoted some combination of surprise, disbelief, and/or annoyance. As for myself, although I have no moral or other objections to physical love in any of its many Earthly, alien and mixed forms, I have always found my best gratification in that creature *woman*. Also, I would dislike being thought of as so foolish that I would select a love partner who came into sexual heat only once every seven years.'

animal passions, hence forever devoting their minds to logic . . .'

The chant of reason was coming to an end and a troubled Spock remained kneeling before the High Master T'sai. Whatever the entity which had invaded Spock's mind this morning, its presence seemed gone now. Perhaps he had misunderstood and had not felt fear – perhaps it had merely been surprise. Even a full Vulcan might be forgiven feeling some surprise over so powerful a consciousness touching his mind. Spock reminded himself that he *had* met every test of *Kolinahr*; the Masters themselves were acknowledging this by their very presence and participation in this ancient ceremony.

Spock could feel that T'sai was turning toward him as the ceremony approached the invitation to mindmeld. He knew that he must accept, and then enter T'sai's mind, and she his. As part of her mind, he would be able to view himself and his place in the universe with the wisdom of a Master. And T'sai would become part of the consciousness that was Spock.

Forget Earth; think only of Vulcan. You were born here of a Vulcan father, raised here as a Vulcan son . . . and Vulcan children like children everywhere can be unthinkingly cruel. Strange I have never been aware until now that it was my boyhood on Vulcan which had ultimately driven me into Starfleet. I had to prove to myself that those times of tears and laughter had been only a child's errors. It was to prove my mastery over myself that I went out among humans and defied them to make me less Vulcan than I am.

But what was it that Jim Kirk had once said? 'Spock, why fight so hard to be a part of only one world? Why not fight instead to be the best of both?'

'Spock!'

This from one of the lesser Masters. T'sai herself was looking down at Spock, puzzled.

'Spock, our minds also have felt that far off "presence". Has it special meaning to you?'

There was nothing Spock could do but to nod . . . *and to feel shame.* Here, now, in the very midst of the *Kolinahr* ceremony, the mysterious alien consciousness was returning to probe his mind again. Again, he felt its interest in Earth . . . and then again he felt fear! And he felt shame, too. As if struck by a bolt from an unseen ambush, Spock knew in this instant that the human half of him was far from extinguished. That half had simply been capable of *human guile* and had learned to hide itself even from his own notice. He had foolishly and carelessly underestimated it and believed it to be gone. But like the enemy it had always been, his human half had merely lain in wait in order to assault him while he was defenseless.

'Spock, your thoughts. Open them to me.'

Spock could not refuse the High Master T'sai, not even at this moment of shame. As she touched him, Spock let his mind open, in the giving and receiving of mindmeld Oneness. *Kaiidth!* What was there was there, and it was T'sai's right to learn the complete truth of it.

The Klingons weren't destroyed. It feels like . . . like they've become 'wall exhibits in Hell'. And it's headed for Earth. Spock, I wish you were here to help me understand.

Spock looked up, puzzled. That had felt like Jim Kirk's thoughts. And yet it was T'sai who was standing here and to whom he had opened his thoughts. She was now releasing Spock's consciousness and retrieving her own. Then her lips opened, and before she spoke Spock already knew what her words would be.

'Your answer lies elsewhere, Spock.'

CHAPTER THREE

Kirk had shuttled immediately across the Med basin to the massive old hydroelectric complex at Gibraltar. Here, Starfleet maintained one of its communications branches from which he could contact headquarters and confirm the senceiver alert.

It was also the fastest way in which he could get another answer. Troubling Kirk almost as much as the mysterious 'cloud intruder' had been the fact that the senceiver message carried no intimation that he was being summoned back to Starfleet Headquarters. He felt that he must have somehow missed that part of the message – otherwise something had to be dreadfully wrong. It was unthinkable that Starfleet, facing an emergency like this, would ignore his years of deep space experience, not to mention his staff responsibilities in areas of fleet deployment.

A troubled Jim Kirk paused outside the Gib signal installation, wanting to compose himself before contacting the Admiralty. He was standing near the top of the massive ramparts which towered high above Gibraltar. Well over twenty kilometers away he could see identical ramparts at the Africa side, and between them the mighty wall separating the Atlantic Ocean from what had once been the Mediterranean Sea. This spectacular panorama, combining as it did with his love of history, began to work on his imagination. Putting all his weight on one foot, Kirk could just barely feel the hum of the huge old hydroelectric turbines which still operated deep down at bedrock level where great streams of cold Atlantic Ocean water plunged sixty meters down to the Mediterranean Sea level. He knew this installation to be hopelessly bulky and inefficient by today's standards, and yet it was still operating – certainly a tribute to the skill of those early twenty-first century engineers whose creation here had served the energy needs of Southern Europe and most of North Africa for almost two centuries.

Below him past the sea-locks, Kirk could make out Gibraltar Rock itself, looking so tiny from here that it was hard to believe it had once been an important military bastion in the power struggles which had divided humanity. The fabled Mediterranean Sea was now hardly more than a long, slender lake which trailed off into the hazy blue distance in the direction from which he had just come. He wondered if the old Mediterranean Alliance had done the right thing in so drastically altering the character of this old sea and the region surrounding it. The Mediterranean had played a significant role in humanity's climb to civilization – did humanity really have the right to meddle to this extent with their past and with the nature of planet Earth? As always, Kirk was forced to admit that the answer was, of course, *yes*. The inescapable fact was that human ingenuity had saved more of the past here than it had lost – the museum cities and the library at Alexandria were only two examples of that. On what had been sea-bottom pre-Minoan ruins had yielded priceless new information on the human past. And the skillfully engineered climate alterations had not only made the entire Med Basin into a virtual garden, it had profoundly improved the climate and the character of the entire northern half of Africa – and this had contributed greatly to that continent's having become an island of human progress and tranquility during the savagery which had racked much of the rest of the world during the twenty-first century.

Kirk became aware of a squawking seagull which in turn made him also aware that for several minutes now he had been standing there gawking and daydreaming like a tourist. He turned and hurried through the signal center entry, annoyed at being so easily distracted. The African vacation leave was over; he could visit and explore the old Gib Complex another time. But now he was a flag officer responding to a major Starfleet alert.

Inside, Kirk found it to be one of those small signal relay stations built in the days when travel around Earth required many more hours than it did now. The young signal technician came to her feet fast, surprised at receiving such a high-ranking visitor, a reaction that changed to something closer to awe as Kirk identified himself.

It was a nuisance having to ask to be put through to Starfleet on a security basis. Kirk considered most secrecy something which usually degraded the accuracy of whatever it touched. The I.D. scan quickly confirmed his identity, and the young technician led him immediately to the security-shielded comcon room.

As Kirk seated himself at the transceiver console, the viewer came on to reveal a comcon operator who smiled pleasantly at Kirk from nearly half a world away in San Francisco.

'Admiral Kirk, operator. Request verification . . .'

'Yes, sir, I understand.' The operator had interrupted Kirk quickly but courteously. 'Please stand by for a moment.'

The operator's image faded from the viewer, and in the same instant the console readouts informed Kirk he was to remain silent until further notice. Clearly, Starfleet wanted no unnecessary conversations about this alert. He heard the hum of an I.D. sensor and realized he was being scanned and his identity verified a second time. Evidently, Starfleet was determined to keep the existence of the Intruder 'cloud' from becoming general knowledge at this time. *Why?* Kirk felt adrenalin surge into his bloodstream as he realized there could be only one possible reason – the Intruder was indeed headed for Earth, and the danger was real enough to cause panic if the information got out before Starfleet was ready with some answers.

Kirk's mind was already racing ahead to consider still other possibilities, too. If the power of the Intruder was as awesome as it had seemed, this could become one of those emergencies in which rules had to change and procedures had to be altered. The right opportunity if resolutely seized might even allow one Admiral James T. Kirk to escape from his flag rank prison.

Until now Kirk had not permitted himself to admit how desperately unhappy he had been during the last couple of years. It was his pride; it was hard to accept the painful truth that his acceptance of admiral's stars had been a foolish blunder, even a ridiculous one considering that his friend and mission comrade, ship's doctor McCoy, had tried so desperately to warn him against accepting flag rank. Bones McCoy had even invaded staff country at the Admiralty, angrily insisting that James Kirk was one of that 'quarterdeck breed' whose symbiotic man-vessel relationship had intrigued and puzzled psychiatrists (and before them, poets) since the days of sailing vessels. To such men, command of a starship is likely to be an ultimate experience – no other way of life, no combination of honors or gratifications can ever come near the excitement, challenges and almost total freedom of a deep space command.

What Kirk did not realize was that the decision to accept admiral's stars had already been made for him by Starfleet's commanding Admiral. On bringing the Enterprise back safely from its historic mission, Kirk had become simply too valuable to be allowed to accept another deep space command. He had not been told that McCoy's arguments had been supported by many medical colleagues who believed that a ground assignment at this juncture might destroy Kirk, or at least his Starfleet career. Starfleet's commanding Admiral had had to make a difficult choice between what was good for Kirk, and what was good for Starfleet – and the organization had won. Kirk was never even aware that he had been cleverly manipulated from the beginning in ways that had made McCoy's arguments seem trivial and made flag rank appear to be new growth and new adventure. Also, he had not really understood how deeply Spock's abrupt departure for Vulcan had affected him. He had been depending on the Vulcan's friendship and logic much more than he realized.

By the time Kirk had recovered from the physical and emotional exhaustion of his five-year mission, he was already an Admiral, a member of the Commanding Admiral's staff, and was convinced that he had simply followed the path of responsibility and duty.

Still seated at the Gibraltar Station signal console, Kirk waited for the San Francisco operator to appear again on his viewer. He was about ready to place his call again when the viewer flickered and the operator's image appeared.

'Gib comcon, I have an Admiralty staff officer requesting holocom contact with you. Stand by, please.'

Vice-Admiral Lori Ciani arrived. It was, of course, only her holocom image, but it was a surprise nevertheless. It was a perfect transmission signal connecting the Gib Station with Starfleet, and she looked so completely real and radiant that Kirk could suddenly hear his heart pounding as it always did whenever she came near to him during that year they had spent together. As always, her unusually large eyes and the slim, youthful angularity in her arms and legs reminded him of a fawn's wild grace and innocence – and he marvelled again at how much this look contrasted with her real wildness which was anything but fawnlike, but much more exciting and satisfying. She was also a remarkably brilliant and able officer, as attested by the fact that she was a member of the Commanding Admiral's inner staff. She was the zenopsychologist in charge of Starfleet Command's relationships with non-human species, and also Nogura's personal representative to the *new human* groups here at home.

'Hello, Jim.' As always, her lips seemed to caress his name as she spoke it.

He could almost catch the scent of her body fragrance and he could feel the slight pressure of his genitals responding to those memories. She had been *perfection* – lover, friend, wife, mother, and in every other role and joy she supplied as he slowly recovered from the fatigue and emotional wounds of those five long years out there. They had lived the basic and simple one year arrange-

27

ment together – but those months had been memorable ones. He had not been aware, at least not consciously, that during that time she had been something of a *surrogate Enterprise* to him.

'What's happening, Lori?'

'Admiral Nogura knew you'd be calling and he asked me to verify the alert.'

Kirk remembered how he had once wondered if the Commanding Admiral had had any hidden motives in bringing Lori and himself together. But he had dismissed the notion as ridiculous. True, living with Lori had helped make a promotion to flag rank seem attractive, even sensible . . .

Lori interrupted his thoughts; 'How well did the implant signal come through?'

'If a huge "cloud" thing just ripped three Klingon heavies apart, I received it fine; someone did a good job of infiltrating our drones into that formation.'

Lori nodded. 'Commander Branch at Epsilon Nine. I have his entire signal ready if you'd like a direct look at it.'

As he started to reply, Kirk became troubled by something she had said earlier. *Admiral Nogura knew you'd be calling and he asked me to verify the alert.* Strange; why would the Commanding Admiral send Lori to do this? The San Francisco comcon operator could have replayed the original signal for him. Certainly, Nogura had more pressing duties for Lori at a time like this.

Lori's holocom image frowned slightly at the play of expression on Kirk's features. Actually, of course, the real Lori Ciana was sitting at a console at Starfleet Headquarters, where she was herself watching a holocom image of Kirk which appeared to be sitting next to her there. That holocom image of him was obviously revealing to her that something was troubling him. 'If you're wondering why fleet deployment hasn't been discussed with you, Jim, it's because the Intruder is headed this way at over warp seven . . .'

'*Warp seven?*' Nothing in the implant alert had suggested this incredible speed – even the deep space Klingon empire was only *days* away at this velocity! Kirk was aghast. Unless fleet deployment had been radically changed recently, Starfleet probably had nothing within interception range of an object moving toward Earth at that velocity.

Lori read this expression too and nodded. 'This is why you haven't been ordered to report here, Jim. We've no deployment to discuss. We haven't even a light cruiser within interception range.'

'Still, there may be something I can . . .'

'Of course, Admiral Nogura is anxious to have the benefit of your space experience,' Lori interrupted. 'Which is why he assigned me to give you a look at the original transmission. Any comments or guesses you might have, I'm to relay them to him immediately.'

For the first time since Kirk had known Lori, he became aware that she was either lying or at least withholding some part of the full truth. Whoever had sent her to do this had miscalculated. Lori might be capable of a good lie if she believed it important and necessary – but plainly she thought this one to be neither. Also, Kirk had learned to know her far too well to be deceived this easily.

'Let's see the transmission,' he said. He could deal with any deception later. Meanwhile, he wanted the best possible look at whatever was headed for Earth.

Lori touched a console control in San Francisco. The images picked up by the outpost's drones and relayed to Earth were clean and nearly perfect.

They were also *frightening*. Kirk's holocom console now seemed to be hurtling through space in the midst of the Klingon cruiser formation. Unlike the senceiver alert, command level holocom images have no 'daydream' quality – they appear in full dimension with a reality which seems actually to surround whoever sits at the receiving holocom console.

'Hold tight, we'll seem to be coming in very close to them.'

It was Lori, her image warning Kirk that the drone sending this particular image was maneuvering to record close detail on the leading cruiser. Despite Lori's warning, Kirk found himself clutching at his armrest as he seemed to hurtle in on a collision course with a huge Klingon vessel. Definitely, these were of the new K't'inga class – Kirk could clearly see the larger engine nacelles, the new clusters of deflector screen pods and the heavier torpedo tubes. In the past, Starfleet's best had proved only marginally superior to earlier Klingon designs and these K't'inga class heavies could signal new problems for Starfleet's present starships.

Then the mysterious 'cloud' thing appeared, driving all thoughts of Klingons from Kirk's mind. The senceiver 'daydream' images had made it seem ominous enough, but this perfect holocom image let Kirk's space-experienced eyes appreciate its true size. Its strange, colorful transluscence could have contained and hidden a hundred planets like Earth . . . perhaps a thousand.

'Our science staff's theory' – this was Lori talking –

'. . . is that the cloud itself may be a powerfield generated by something inside at the heart of it.'

'Shit!' It was an expression that a very young Jim Kirk had learned from Grandfather Samuel. It seemed to fit this moment exactly. Kirk's mind reeled at the incredible power that would be needed to generate a powerfield that size. He wondered if even the sun generated power on that scale.

Then the holocom images faded and he no longer seemed to be hurtling through space. The signal stations' walls reappeared – Lori's image remained – and apparently his own image was still seated next to her in San Francisco since she seemed still to be watching him. Was she awaiting his response to what they had just seen? Or to what had been left unsaid?

Come on, Lori, image or not, I can see that you've got something troubling to say. But you've always had a way of making troubling things seem sensible, haven't you? Is this the first time Nogura has sent you to me this way?

'Jim, there is one starship that might be . . . positioned in time to pull of an interception.'

Kirk understood completely. But he kept his expression blank. *Your next words could brand you a whore, Lori. Nogura's staff whore. I hope to God I'm wrong.*

'The Enterprise, Jim. There's a chance they can get her out of oribital dockyards in time.'

'And?' Whatever Nogura had sent her here to say, he wasn't going to help her with it.

'The commanding admiral . . .'

'Meaning Nogura, of course . . .'

'Of course. He's ordered everyone available from your old crew aboard. That will give Captain Decker the best . . .'

'Captain Decker?'

'Yes, you recommended they give the Enterprise to him, didn't you? He'll have the top crew in Starfleet, people already accustomed to working together . . .'

'And Nogura was worried that I might want to take her out myself?'

'Well . . . no. Certainly, you'll agree that the Enterprise has been so completely rebuilt and refitted that she's not the same ship you were so familiar with. Your protégé . . .'

'Decker.'

'Yes, he's been aboard eighteen months now; he's intimately familiar with every change . . .'

'He knows the design changes, her new systems, like no one in the Fleet could possibly know them.'

'That's right, Jim.'

'Thank you, Lori. Mind if I close down this console now? I've an appointment and I'm already running late on it.'

CHAPTER FOUR

Whatever one prefers to call it – Starfleet Command, Fleet Headquarters, or the Admiralty – it is centered in a structure which thrusts itself magnificently spaceward out of the redwood forest of San Francisco's old city peninsula. Although some museum cities have taller buildings preserved from the industrial past, Starfleet's headquarters are still a distinctive landmark in this world where so much of the clutter of our lives has been placed underground.

Just under two hours ago, Kirk had taken the tube from Gibraltar to Los Angeles Island where he had caught the first northbound airtram. Now, fifteen minutes later, the clear blue waters of San Francisco Bay were in full view. As always, the sight of Starfleet's headquarters seemed to make Kirk's heart beat a bit faster. Since his midshipman days, he had always admired the clean symmetry of the design and its dramatic combination of space and Earth materials. There was an almost story-book castle suggestion in the way its tritanium blue superstructure rose up out of its grey-granite base. It had always been to Kirk a statement in architectural poetry about a very necessary relationship between the mud below and the stars above.

Today, however, no such thoughts entered Kirk's mind. He was an angry and disillusioned man, with much of the anger and bitterness directed at himself. How was it possible he could have spent almost three years so totally blind to the fact that the Commanding Admiral had been manipulating him?

'Starfleet in three minutes.'

It was the computer's routine announcement, signalling descent. Below them Kirk could make out the sparse line of slender pylons whose microwaves beamed power and guidance up to the tram.

In only a few minutes, he would begin a confrontation that would decide whether he remained in Starfleet, or lived, or died, or even gave a damn which of these happened. The key was Commanding Admiral Heihachiro Nogura. Kirk had no doubts left about why Nogura had ordered Lori Ciana to make her holocom visit to Gibraltar. Faced with all the pressures of the Intruder emergency, the Commanding Admiral had hurriedly assigned Lori to placate a potentially troublesome James Kirk. Nogura must have assumed that since she had managed Kirk so well once, she would find a way to do it again. But this time Kirk had finally felt himself being manipulated.

Does familiarity breed contempt even within Admiralties? Perhaps as the last couple of years passed, a deskbound and miserable James Kirk had seemed easier and easier to manipulate. There had been nothing recently that would remind Nogura, or even Lori, that he was still the same man listed so prominently in the Enterprise logbook. Perhaps he really hadn't been the same man – at least not until now.

To Kirk, it was as if he had unexpectedly been given the full use of his eyes and ears again. And his full mind. How incredible it was that he had stopped analyzing, questioning, doubting! In deep space it would have cost lives, perhaps his entire vessel. Here, he had not even

34

noticed that Nogura had been using him.* How could he have missed seeing it? From the day he had brought his battered starship and crew back from their long mission, Kirk had become uniquely valuable to Nogura. Not to *Nogura the man*, kindly, a great-great grandfather a dozen times over and a helpful friend since Kirk's junior lieutenant days. Kirk's value was to Heihachiro Nogura, Commanding Admiral, whose oath it was to make any sacrifice or pay any price necessary to fulfilling his responsibilities to his beloved Starfleet.

The *new humans* among Earth's population had become increasingly critical of Starfleet's cost, of its aims, and of its value. Admiral Nogura could not avoid seeing immediately the value of a living symbol, a carefully designed hero figure who could awe the impressionable and confront the critics with arguments taken from actual experiences out there. And Starfleet needed that hero symbol *here*, not out of sight somewhere on another long starship mission.

Alcatraz Children's Park had hardly slipped past view on the left when Kirk felt the tram's inertia-dampeners hum into life – there was no motion sensation at all as the tram dipped sharply to the right, decelerating fast. He caught a quick glimpse of the mirror-blue of the Admiralty towering high above them, and then suddenly the tram was through the Telegraph Hill entry and was settling to a stop at the terminal beneath Starfleet Headquarters.

* ADMIRAL KIRK'S COMMENT: The fact that Nogura 'used' me (and Admiral Lori Ciana, too) is no more shocking to me today than my memory of the times I have been forced to risk the safety and lives of my own subordinates when I believed it necessary to the safety of our vessel and crew. Ours is a difficult service and the job of command can be the loneliest and most painful of all tasks.

Kirk was the first out, hurrying through the high domed interior, oblivious to the striking view of San Francisco Bay through the broad tram entry opening. The place was busy, and only later would Kirk remember that most of the facial expressions here, at least the human ones which could be read, were somber and worried. He was unconscious of the fact that his own center of interest had changed completely in the last few hours. Although he still believed he had hurried here out of professional concern over the mysterious Intruder, his inner mind was increasingly thinking of a vessel called *Enterprise*.

'Commander Sonak!'

Sonak turned, startled to have his name called in public – on Vulcan it would have been a shameful breach of privacy. The Vulcan fleet scientist was still more startled to see that it was Kirk, who certainly knew and respected Vulcan tastes. He knew that some extraordinary urgency could be responsible for such discourtesy.

'Have you received your appointment as Enterprise Science Officer?'

The Vulcan nodded. 'Based, I am told, on your recommendation, Admiral. Thank you.'

The 'thank you' was unnecessary but Sonak added it nevertheless. This human, Kirk, had many times demonstrated himself worthy of respect.

'Then why aren't you on board?'

Sonak closed his mind to this offensive directness. 'Captain Decker requested I complete final science briefing here before . . .'

Kirk interrupted. 'Here at Starfleet? The Enterprise is in final preparation to leave dock . . .'

36

'Which will require at least *twenty* more hours at minimum, Admiral.'

'She'll leave in *twelve* hours,' corrected Kirk. 'Report to me aboard as soon as possible.'

'To *you*, sir?'

Kirk nodded firmly. 'I intend to have a brief meeting with Nogura, after which I will go directly to the Enterprise.'

Then Kirk turned and strode away, hurrying toward the turbolifts. The Vulcan gazed after him, lifting an eyebrow quizzically. Had this seemed a slightly different Kirk from the one Sonak had known previously? He wished that humans were not such an enigma.

If Kirk had thought of the Enterprise before, it had been as an impossible dream. Starship command was a way of life that no flag officer could never again enjoy, at least so long as that officer stayed in Starfleet. Eventually, the thought of resignation from the service would have come to Kirk's mind – although he could never know the incredible freedom and independence of starship command again, there were many other worlds with other kinds of vessels out there.

As Kirk made his way to Nogura's office, the Enterprise was very much in his thoughts again. He had no idea, however, how much the need for the Starship was motivating him. He sincerely believed that he came here because an emergency existed and Enterprise was needed – and that he, Kirk, was a better choice to command her than the admittedly talented but much less experienced Decker.

'This must be rather difficult for you,' said Nogura.

'Captain Decker has been something of your protégé, hasn't he?'

'Yes, sir, but I don't see how that makes it difficult. I've recommended him for jobs in the past because he was the best man available. In this case, he is not.'

Kirk knew himself to be motivated and determined as he had not been for years – and he had powerful arguments to use. The last five years of Enterprise logs supported his contention that Nogura's greatest need was *not* a Captain familiar with a rebuilt vessel but rather one with the greatest possible experience in dealing with deep space unknowns such as the one now hurtling toward Earth.

At first Nogura had seemed indifferent and impatient but Kirk had seen that the Commanding Admiral was also troubled and tired. Logs aside, was *today's* Kirk a better Captain than the alert and upcoming young Decker? How much had Kirk been damaged by almost three years on the ground in an unfamiliar and unhappy environment? Ordinarily, Kirk would never have risked this direct a confrontation with the Commanding Admiral. But this was the first real challenge Kirk had faced in these past three years and Nogura, however dynamic and fearsome his personality, was also the man who had manipulated him, used him. This was a battle that Kirk was determined to win.

Kirk could see that Nogura was beginning to question the decision to use Decker, being unusually patient, incredibly so considering his reputation. It was becoming obvious that he must feel genuine regret over the way he had forced Kirk into flag rank.

Kirk had been with Nogura for twelve minutes. He had never known a visitor or decision here to last that long. Then, he felt a chill as Nogura came abruptly to his feet.

'The entire staff considered this at length, Jim,' said Nogura. 'I'm afraid that every point you've made has already been carefully considered.'

'Admiral, these points were *neither* carefully nor properly considered since I was not present.' Kirk knew that his only chance now was to challenge Nogura directly. 'And now that I am present, I submit that it is your responsibility to inform me of whatever negative arguments were made against my selection.'

As a flag officer *and* a member of Nogura's staff, Kirk had both a right and an obligation to know of anything in his professional performance which his peers considered to be substandard.

Nogura's eyes remained fixed on Kirk's as five seconds passed, then ten . . . twenty . . . Kirk fought to keep the slightest expression off his own face. He sensed that everything would be won or lost now in the next minute.

'How badly do you want her back?'

'The Enterprise? I can't deny it'll be pleasant to be back aboard her . . .'

'Jim, I am placing you on your honor. If there is the slightest chance that you are being motivated by *anything* other than professional considerations of intercepting whatever this is, trying to identify it, making contact with any life forms involved . . .'

'I don't understand the reference to *honor*, Heihachiro. I don't recall ever lying to you in the past – and I'm certain you never have to me.'

Kirk knew that he had won. He also believed that everything he had said or left unsaid was the whole and complete truth.

CHAPTER FIVE

Kirk strode through Starfleet headquarters to the main orbital transporter, trying to keep elation off his face. He knew that he had taken shameless advantage of Heihachiro Nogura's decency. But he was satisfied that it was for good reason. He was thinking of Nogura's final words: *If you are convinced that you are the right man, Jim, then go! If you are not, then for God's sake don't!*

Had McCoy been present, he would have been concerned. This was not the Kirk of the Enterprise logs, not completely at any rate. Something was gone, some edge had been blunted, and at this moment there was no way to know whether it could be repaired again or not. This Kirk's mind was on the Enterprise, and only secondarily on the 'cloud' Intruder headed toward Earth. McCoy might have warned him that while the love of man for a vessel and the love for a woman will rarely bear more than poetic comparison, they do both share a similar passion for *possession* – and also a similar blindness toward the *responsibilities* which this entails.

Kirk stepped onto the transporter platform. 'Navy yards. Centroplex, area seven. Energize.'

The transporter deposited Kirk in an engineering arm of the enormous Centroplex which housed administration and most of the other central needs of the vast, sprawling orbital dockyard. It was Starfleet's largest ship construction and repair facility this side of Antares. It was here almost nine years ago that a younger Captain James Kirk had first taken command of the Enterprise.

Chief Engineer Montgomery Scott saw Kirk and with a look of pleased surprise he broke away from a group at an engineering computer. Scott's dark eyes and firm mouth behind the new moustache flashed a quick acknowledgement of past years together, but his expression still reflected worried concern.

'Admiral, these departure orders. Starfleet canna be serious.'

'Why aren't the Enterprise transporters operating, Mister Scott?'

'A temporary problem, sir.' Then quickly, getting his point in, 'Admiral, we've just been through eighteen months of redesigning and refitting. We might have launched in twenty hours. But who the hell's idea was it to suddenly have her ready in *twelve* hours?'

Kirk could see that this meeting with Scotty was being watched curiously. The place must be crawling with rumors and his arrival up here would no doubt start an eddy of new ones, some of these possibly accurate. He motioned to Scott, moving him toward the circular pneumatic doors leading to a travel pod attached to the outside of the Centroplex.

Scott's eyes narrowed. He had spent too many years with Kirk not to be aware that something was up. Then he recognized the look; he had seen this expression on Kirk's features a few times before. Scott's former Captain was readying himself to face trouble with someone, but it was a fight he was determined to win. The Chief Engineer began treading carefully, but not dropping the subject which worried him. 'She needs more work, a shakedown . . .'

'Let's go,' Kirk said flatly.

Scott blinked in surprise, uncertain for a moment what he was being asked to do. But Kirk was entering the travel pod and Scott realized he had just been directed to take Kirk over to the Enterprise. It had been no request; it was an order.

'Aye, sir.' Scott moved quickly to the travel pod controls where he punched in his identity number and their destination. Behind them, both the Centroplex seal and the travel pod doors snapped shut and the hydraulic bolts clanged shut.

Kirk moved up to the front of the pod with Scott. The green disengage light – then the slightest jar as the travel pod was released from the huge Centroplex. They were floating free now, Scott playing its thruster controls like a three finger exercise as he took them out into the half-light over the orbital dockyards. Earth was above and to one side of them, its enormous bulk backlit by the sun which was disappearing across the vast smooth expanse of the Pacific.

Kirk spoke rapidly, filling Scott in on the pertinent details of the command alert – he described the luminescent 'cloud' and Starfleet's belief that it might actually be a *powerfield* effect being produced by some incredible energy source at the heart of the 'cloud'. Scott looked up sharply at Kirk's description of the new class Klingon cruisers, then his eyes flashed a signal of mixed satisfaction and concern as Kirk sketched the Klingon destruction. The two men's eyes met; it was satisfying to know that the most powerful vessels in the Klingon fleet were destructible, but this left hanging the unanswered (and presently unanswerable) question of whether the redesigned Enterprise would weather an attack from the Intruder any better.

'The Klingons had definitely attacked it first,' Kirk said. 'The Enterprise won't make that mistake, of course . . .'

'There is no guaranteeing what the Enterprise will do,' interrupted Scott. 'No one's even sure what she's *capable* of doing. The engines, the deflectors, weapons and defense systems, it's *all* new. Not even a shakedown cruise, much less any battle tests! And the *engines*, Admiral, they're yet to be even tested at warp power. Add to that an inexperienced captain . . .'

Kirk interrupted. 'Two and a half years in Starfleet operations may have made me a little stale, Mister Scott, but I wouldn't exactly consider myself "inexperienced".'

It took Scott a moment to comprehend – then a long, sharp look at Kirk's expression to make doubly certain. Flag officers did not normally return to single-vessel command.

'They gave her back to me, Scotty.'

Scott peered at him, comprehending some and guessing the rest. ' "*Gave*" her back, sir? I doubt it was that easy.' Scott had no doubts but that it was Kirk himself who had pulled this off. 'Any man who could manage such a feat I wouldn't dare disappoint,' continued Scott. 'She'll launch on time, sir. I'll get her ready somehow.'

Kirk simply nodded. He expected that much and would be satisfied with nothing less. Meanwhile, his eyes had begun scanning out to the side in the direction in which the orbital travel pod was moving. He realized that Scott had purposely been keeping a part of the dockyards out of sight during the past conversation.

Kirk's expression softened; he could see a look of pride coming on to Scott's face. There was a touch of pleasure there, too, as he touched a lateral thruster control.

'There she is, sir!'

43

CHAPTER SIX

She hung there inside the lacy filigree of the orbital dry dock. *Enterprise!*

Montgomery Scott, with some unexpected flair for drama, had maneuvered to keep the starship from Kirk's sight until the last possible moment. Then, he had used the lateral thruster to nudge their travel pod into a sweeping turn, bringing Enterprise into glorious full view.

Kirk's eyes saw only her. It was as if the delicate latticework structure around the starship did not exist – or if he was aware of the dry dock at all, he saw it and its lights as bejeweled space-sculpture existing only to frame and highlight the new symmetry and breathtaking beauty of Enterprise.

The dramatic impact was heightened by the light which flooded her from every angle within the huge orbital dock, seemingly doubly brilliant against the velvet blackness of space beyond. Kirk had, of course, seen some of her new lines before but only at a mid-point in the renovation. She was complete now, gracefully whole – Kirk searched for some phrase, some description that expressed what he was feeling. Was she like a lovely woman? No, at this moment she was more than that to him. A fable? A myth come alive? Yes, that was it! She was as Aphrodite must have been when Zeus first raised her up from the sea, naked and shockingly beautiful.

'Raised up *who*, sir?' It was Scott giving him a puzzled look. Kirk realized he must have said some part of that aloud.

Scott had steered their pod along the length of her and breadth of her, allowing Kirk to savor every view – and the chief engineer was tactful enough to point out enough design changes and details to maintain the fiction of this being merely an inspection look. But now their pod's control monitor was flashing the symbols which assigned them to use one of the airlocks at a cargo deck.

Kirk felt the pod mating home, the metallic sound of security bolts locking and the familiar pneumatic whoosh of the air-lock doors opening.

You can go home again! Whoever denied that had been wrong! And now, what was it Scotty was saying?

'Welcome aboard, Captain,' repeated Scott.

The cargo deck was a confusion of supplies and equipment, zero-g cargo carriers, and hurrying technicians. Kirk felt apprehensive when he saw how completely redesigned she was even here. Neither his study of the design prints nor his visits during construction had prepared him for the sheer multitude of changes which her final form carried now. But even in the confusion here, he could begin to discern those patterns of activity which come only from careful design planning – there was something comfortably sensible in the way these odd shaped new cargo containers traveled along on zero-gravity sleds, almost as if ignoring the scattered, perspiring crewmen, each container like an intelligent jigsaw puzzle piece capable of finding its own planned storage place in the vessel.

The airlocks behind Kirk and Scott had clanged shut – the travel pod which brought them here was needed elsewhere in some part of the orbital dockyard. There was hurry and signs of fatigue among the work crews here as they struggled to have their part of the Enterprise ready in the near-impossible time of twelve hours.

Could she be gotten out in time? Somewhere inside the vessel here was Captain Decker who had argued to Starfleet that a bare dozen hours were not enough. And Decker knew this Enterprise — there could be no doubt but that he must know her intimately by now. Could he, Kirk, do what young and capable Decker said was impossible?

A perspiring young ensign was coming forward to greet them, suddenly nervous at the sight of an Admiral having come aboard. *Lord, how young they were making them these days*.

'Permission to come aboard, sir,' Kirk said.

'Granted, sir,' the ensign said. 'Welcome aboard, Admiral . . . and Commander Scott, you're needed in Engineering immediately.'

'Sir, if you'll excuse me?' said Scott, hurrying off. *The full impact of all this hit Kirk again. I'm back!* In the same instant, he became aware that his presence here was complicating the life of a very harried young ensign who clearly had other jobs needing his attention, too.

'Sir, if there's somewhere you'd like to be escorted . . .'

'I think I can find my own way, Ensign.' Kirk moved off, feeling the young officer's relief at his back. He moved across a catwalk and then crossed the open deck toward the nearest turbolift. He waited a few seconds and then began to wonder if the lifts featured some redesign that required he do more than stand within sensor range. He searched his mind rapidly for any memory of any such redesign in Enterprise's turbolifts . . .

The turbolift cab arrived; it had the familiar old *whoosh* sound as it opened. Kirk stepped inside, drinking in the sensation of being there and of giving the voice command which came next.

'Bridge,' he ordered, savoring the moment.

The turbolift mechanisms responded; engaged and began to move more quickly than he remembered. He could feel just the slightest residue of undampened inertia which told him of the cab's rapid acceleration upward, and then the slightest feeling of sliding sideways as the turbolift traveled horizontally to enter another shaft before continuing up again. On the wall of the cab there was a new style turbolift position readout but he gave it only a glance since his own trained senses told him all that he needed to know – the lift had passed through the starship's great engineering section and it was now streaking up inside the broad support pylon toward the saucer section. Yes, there was the faintest feeling of acceleration now as it shot up through the first eleven decks toward the bridge level.

Deceleration! He was a couple of seconds from being there. Would the bridge crew have been informed that he was her Captain again? Either way, his first impression on them would be important. He should appear intelligently concerned but also determined and confident that they would give him their full . . .

The turbolift door snapped open. Kirk stepped out onto the bridge, his entry unnoticed and his presence unrecognized. Unlike the cargo deck's vast arena of confusion, the bridge here was more like a pressure pot at full boil. Disarray everywhere; test equipment underfoot, consoles open, viewing screens disconnected, relays clocking, servos whining, and somewhere an overload signal protesting with its nerve-jangling warning squeal.

Again Kirk felt apprehension – a sensation of having come into this perhaps too precipitously, possibly even too unprepared. Characteristically he was immediately angry at himself for permitting negative thoughts – command was a *positive* function! He had visited here during refit; carefully looked over all her new design plans and specs. He'd make himself at home here and fast! Some of this disarray was already beginning to make sense to him.

They had begun to see him. The Asian romantic Sulu, lieutenant commander's stripes now, stood sweat-soaked at the helm where he had frozen in mid-motion as he saw Kirk. Uhura, also a lieutenant commander, the same classically lovely features, abruptly stopping in the midst of a flurry of hailing frequency checks. And Chekov, appearing almost too boyish to be a full lieutenant, at the complex new weapons-control station. Kirk remembered hearing that Chekov had recently returned from weapons-defense command school.

'Sir . . . ?'

'You over there, kill that over-load signal!'

A hush began to fall, the fact of Kirk's presence carried one to another by looks and quick murmurs. There was no questioning the delight and welcome on Uhura's face. Then she used the word that he had hoped someone would use. 'Captain,' she said, 'Starfleet just signalled your transfer of command.'

Uhura moving toward him now, Sulu and Chekov too, grins on their faces. Murmured welcomes from some of the new people, too. Kirk became aware that it could quickly become a sentimental and time-consuming welcome. These first moments of taking command were too important for that.

'I appreciate the welcome; I wish the circumstances were less critical.' His tone and the look delivered the

48

message he intended. Time for handshakes and senti-
mentality later. He turned to Uhura: 'Outpost station
Epsilon Nine is monitoring the Intruder. Keep a channel
open to them.'

'Aye, sir,' said Uhura.

Kirk looked around the bridge again, then asked,
'Where is Captain Decker?'

Sulu broke the hush that followed, 'He's in engineering,
sir.' The helmsman indicated the captain's seat. 'He
doesn't know.'

Kirk turned to Chekov. 'Please assemble the full crew
on the Rec Deck at 0400 hours. See that the large viewer
there is hooked up and working. I want to show everyone
what we're facing.'

CHAPTER SEVEN

After the turbolift doors closed behind Kirk there was a lull on the bridge before work was resumed. It was as if his presence had left an electric charge lingering there. Chekov was surprised that he had been holding his breath for some reason.

'He wanted her back,' said Sulu. 'I wouldn't have wanted to be in his way when he went after her!'

Uhura nodded. This was exactly what she had just seen and felt in Kirk, too. He had also had that look which comes into some men's eyes when they've just won a woman and she lies there ready to be taken. Uhura was not unaquainted with that look, but she was troubled at the amount of hunger she had seen there, too.

One of the new relief crew members spoke up, perturbed. 'And Captain Decker? This ship was given to *him* – he's been with her every minute of refitting.'

Uhura's doubts evaporated as she turned to Kirk's defense, her tone brittle. 'Ensign, our chances of getting back from this mission may have just doubled!' Privately she wondered if that would prove good enough. From what she was overhearing on communications, Uhura could piece together a fairly accurate picture of what they faced and she was surprised to find herself wondering if *today's* Jim Kirk could handle that emergency as well as the captain she remembered. There was no denying that he had been three years Earthbound in a job he should never have accepted.

Montgomery Scott stood in the midst of what to many would have seemed pandemonium. The engine's intermix chamber, extending three ship levels above him and four more below, did not yet show the blinding, hellfire look it would have when delivering warp power, but even at this low setting, the flare of the wave-energy collectors gave everything an unearthly appearance. But Scott had long ago learned how to ignore all this. Any other way of working here would have been impossible, although not nearly as impossible as it would have been to him to work elsewhere.

Scott had no dream of one day commanding a starship of his own. Indeed, he would have considered it a foolish waste of his talents. He could conceive of no higher honor or greater glory than was already his as *Chief Engineer* of a starship, and particularly of this one.

The last three years of redesigning and rebuilding her had been the happiest time in Scott's life – and it was being marred now by the fact that they were improperly hurrying his vessel into service. The new design engines had yet to be warp tested, and these engines were *six times as powerful as anything ever carried into space before* – most emphatically they were not things to be hurriedly or carelessly used.

'Ready, Engineer. Let's compare mag-patterns.'

The words came from a well-muscled young torso which, at this moment, appeared to be headless. Actually, Will Decker had managed to work his blond head completely into the tiny access hatch of the auxiliary power console – which was fortunate since it had enabled the young Captain to see the nearly microscopic quadister burn-out which had kept the ship's transporters out of action. It had been a message to this effect which had brought Scott hurrying here from the cargo deck boarding area -- and he was now impressed all over again by Decker's resourcefulness in tracking down and locating the trouble.

Their test patterns compared perfectly, but as Decker carefully worked his head free, his eyes still carried a worried look. The transporters would now begin beaming personnel and cargo up to the ship again, but Decker wished they had time for further overload tests. Why had this particular burn-out occurred and why hadn't it shown up in the tests? Scott, with some of the same doubts, started to suggest that they investigate further -- and then suddenly realized Decker would soon be gone. He found himself feeling increasingly sickhearted over the shattering disappointment in store for this young man whom he had come to like and to respect.

As he saw Kirk come in and move toward them, Scott felt his face flushing in embarrassment as he realized that Kirk was going to say it to Decker *here*. He wondered if he himself should have given the young captain some warning. But no, it would have been improper coming from anyone but Kirk. And in view of their near impossible schedule, Kirk was undoubtedly right in doing it immediately and here, cleanly. If Enterprise was to be ready in only eleven hours now, none of them could let anything take an unnecessary minute of their time.

'Admiral Kirk,' said Captain Willard Decker, pleased, reaching out for a handshake. 'We're getting a top brass sendoff.' The young Captain's self-assured grin reminded Scott of another young Enterprise Captain he had once known. 'She'll launch on schedule if we have to tow her out with our bare hands. Right, Scotty?'

'Aye, sir,' Scott said lamely. 'That we will.'

Kirk broke in, firmly: 'Will, let's step over here and talk.' He indicated a bulkhead corner and Decker looked back at him, puzzled. Then he turned to Scott. 'Let me know when the back-ups are in place.'

'Aye, sir,' Scott said glumly to their backs as the two walked away, Decker almost too handsome, some said, moving with the loose easiness of youth; Kirk more seasoned, with a controlled grace, looking grimly determined to do what he must now do. A simile came to Scott's mind, but he brushed the absurd comparison away immediately – he saw no reason to be reminded of the herd bull returning to find a young usurper rutting there.

'All due respect, sir, I hope this isn't a Starfleet pep talk; I'm just too busy.' Decker said it pleasantly but still firmly. As much as he admired and owed this man whose protégé he had been, his friendship with Kirk had to come second after his own responsibilities here.

'I'm taking the center seat,' Kirk said. 'I'm sorry, Will.'

'You are what . . .?' Decker was certain that Kirk must have said something else.

'I'm replacing you as Captain of the Enterprise.'

Decker found himself staring at Kirk blankly. He saw Kirk reach tentatively as if to clasp a hand on his shoulder, fatherly, brotherly . . . but then Kirk's expression seemed to harden and he drew back. 'You'll stay aboard as Executive Officer . . . a temporary grade reduction to Commander.'

Decker found his voice. 'You *personally* are assuming command?'

'Yes.'

'May I ask why?'

Kirk nodded. 'My experience – five years out there dealing with unknowns like this – my familiarity with the Enterprise, this crew.'

'Admiral, this is an almost totally new Enterprise. You don't know her a tenth as well as I do.' *And you won't have time to get acquainted with her! In thirty hours we could be at battle stations.*

'That's why you're staying aboard,' Kirk answered evenly. 'I'm sorry, Will.'

'No, Admiral,' Decker flared, 'I don't think you *are*; not one damned bit. I remember when you recommended me for this command. You told me how envious you were, and how painful it was to have no way to get a starship command again. Well, sir, it looks like you found a way!'

'Report to the bridge, Commander,' Kirk said flatly. 'Immediately.'

Decker's eyes remained locked with Kirk's for a moment, then he turned stiffly and left.

Kirk watched Decker go and stood collecting his own composure for a moment. He was less dissatisfied with Decker's reaction than with his own handling of it. He felt that he should have been able to make it clear that envy had played no part in taking command of Enterprise again. It had nothing to do with envy . . .

'*What the hell?!*' He had just started across to Scott when he saw the flare of cross-circuiting. It was from the panel that Scott and Decker had been working on.

A technician had pounced on the omnicon switch: 'Transporter room, come in! Urgent!' he shouted, turning to Scott. 'Redline on the transporters, Mister Scott!'

Scott was white-faced, sending the same warning by intercom: 'Transporter room, do not engage! *DO NOT*—'

The technician pointed to a reading. *'Too late. They're beaming up someone now!'*

Kirk and Scott raced for the nearest turbolift.

Transporter Chief Janice Rand had never felt horror like this. Out on the transporter platform there were fluttering swirls of black ugliness, where two crew arrivals should be materializing. Had she made some foolish mistake with her energy-convert setting?

'Go to emergency power source,' she snapped. Her transporter assistant made the switch-over smoothly.

Through the protective shielding, Rand could see the two shapes that seemed to try to materialize, but the patterns were still fluttering – were they also becoming slightly distorted? *What was wrong? She could see now that every control was properly set, all instrument readings were perfect – why were warning lights flashing there now? Her transporter assistant was as perplexed as she was! Damn an untested ship!*

'Starfleet!' She was snapping into the transceiver, 'Override us! OVERRIDE. Yank them back!'

'Unable to retrieve their patterns, Enterprise,' Starfleet was answering.

The two forms were materializing more solidly now. One was a male, a Vulcan apparently. This would be Commander Sonak whom Rand knew was due aboard. The other was younger, an attractive female – Rand felt a new wave of horror as they fluttered from sight again, then reappeared, their bodies clearly misshapen now.

Kirk entered at full run. Scott, only a few steps behind, took over from the transporter assistant as Rand made room for Kirk who began a fast polarity-check of the master controls. She felt some faint relief over the certainty that Jim Kirk would do whatever was possible.

'Damn!' This from Kirk who had reached for the pattern-enhancement boost and had discovered its position changed on this new panel.

'We're losing the pattern.' Scott said it rapidly.

Kirk found the pattern booster control, pushed it to full emergency as he turned to the transceiver: 'Starfleet, boost your matter gain down there; we need more signal!'

Starfleet's response was immediate; there was a flutter of greater solidity on the transporter platforms. The two figures almost fully patterned for an instant – and Rand heard the sound of agony, a disbelieving moan from someone. On the platform? *It was the Captain!*

Kirk fought to keep from screaming obscenities. *It was Lori there! Sonak, too – but what was Lori doing up here? She must have taken a temporary rank reduction to fill the zeno-psychology vacancy aboard. And now she was dying. And he was helpless to stop it!*

'Oh, no. They're forming again!' Rand recognized this as her own voice. Shapes were materializing on the platform again – *but frighteningly misshapen, writhing masses of chaotic flesh with skeletal shapes and pumping organs on the outsides of the 'bodies'. A twisted clawlike hand tore at the air, a scream came from a bleeding mouth* . . . and then they were gone. The chamber was empty.

'Oh my God.' Rand recognized the voice again as being from Kirk. 'Starfleet, do you have them?'

Starfleet came in. The voice was unsteady but quiet. 'Enterprise, what we got back . . . didn't live long. Fortunately.'

Another moment of stunned silence. Then Kirk hit the

button, fighting to control his voice. 'Starfleet; Kirk. Please . . . express my condolences to Commander Ciana's mother and father; say I'll visit them when . . . when circumstances permit. Commander Sonak's family can be reached through the Vulcan Embassy.'

Kirk turned and saw in Rand's face the torment inside. Had *she* killed them?

'There was nothing you could have done, Rand. It wasn't your fault.' Then he turned and left the transporter room.

CHAPTER EIGHT

Kirk moved blindly through the corridor. He hardly saw the hurrying crew and dockyard technicians as they moved aside out of his way. He fought to clear his mind of the image of that distorted thing which had been a woman named Lori. Could he have saved her if he hadn't lost that split-second looking for the new pattern booster switch?

'*Lori*. She must have volunteered, last minute. Had·she discovered they needed an officer trained in her zenopsych specialty? Or had she come hoping for – what? His forgiveness? He hoped that hadn't been it, since she had done him no injury. That first year back on Earth he had needed exactly what she had been to him. She had·realized that too, and it had pleased her immensely to both heal and pleasure him so. The fact that the old fox Nogura had used her took none of that away.

Even as these thoughts passed through Kirk's mind, the old habits of command were returning, demanding that he set aside personal agony. *The effect of this on his vessel, on the mission? Sonak was the critical loss. He was the second best Science Officer in the Fleet. No, the best on active duty.*

Kirk looked up in confusion, then embarrassment – he had lost his way. A passing yeoman stopped in response to his puzzled look. 'Turboshaft eight?' he asked, feeling the fool.

'Back that way, sir,' the yeoman said, pointing toward the way he had come.

*

With the crew exhausted already, concern over these transporter deaths could run through the ship like a shock wave. Despite all its safety back-ups, the transporter had malfunctioned badly. What other systems might fail? Would this shake confidence in the new design? Or confidence in him, now the new Captain? *Should* he launch on schedule with the ship this unready? Decker had been right – she was not the Enterprise that Kirk had once known so intimately. Would Decker's knowledge of her have prevented the accident?

Decker! He was standing there by the turbolift, watching curiously as Kirk approached. Had he seen his replacement having to ask the location of the turbolift shaft?

'We'll have to replace Commander Sonak,' said Kirk. 'But I'd still like a Vulcan there, if possible.'

'None available, Captain.' Did Decker know this for certain? Could he have checked on this already? 'There's no one, in fact, who's *fully* rated on this design.'

'*You* are, Mister Decker,' Kirk said. 'I'm afraid you'll have to double as Science Officer.'

Kirk moved on, feeling Decker's eyes on his back. Was the new Exec waiting for him to fall on his face? Wouldn't he, Kirk, have been resentful if years ago someone had snatched away *his* first command? Kirk thought probably so. Decker's resentment could begin to affect his performance as Exec and as Science Officer too. Had he loaded too much responsibility on Decker?

Kirk was aware that he needed McCoy. Was he being unfair to Decker? Certainly, he was being unfair to himself. He had many times solved problems greater than any Exec could create. And anyway, Decker might create no problems at all – he was a brilliant and responsible young officer. If Kirk was indeed the right Captain for this mission, Decker would begin to see that. But he also knew that Nogura had manipulated him with almost ridiculous ease; and beyond that he knew that he had been out of the center seat for almost three years now. Could he again become that starship captain he used to be? Or could that be delusion too? Was it possible he had just been lucky?

Kirk patched his intercom through to Scott. 'I need a *working* transporter, Engineer! Total checkout and fail-safe backup of any questionable part. Full safety trials before each beam-up. Kirk out.' He had less than ten hours before launch, and then only another twenty-two hours before they would reach and intercept the Intruder – assuming no engine problems. Could he mold this ship, crew and himself into a starworthy unit in that limited time?

Kirk switched his viewer to a look at the Rec Deck and saw that only a few of the crew were early for the 0400 assembly which he had ordered. He made a random ship scan and his spirits were buoyed somewhat as he saw that most of the crew were staying at their launch preparation tasks until the last possible minute.

He could not recall that any starship captain had ever assembled a full crew as he planned to do. There would not have been adequate space for it in earlier design vessels anyway. And there was usually no need for it – a starship's 'nerve system' of computer-regulated scanners and viewers permitted instant contact with anyone at any time. But this case was unique – it needed the crew and Captain face-to-face. They would be seeing the gigantic size of the Intruder's powerfield (if indeed that was its explanation); they would also see the awesome weaponry that had destroyed the Klingons, and instinct told Kirk that in a moment like this, the crew needed to be with the man who would be leading them. And it was important that he be able to measure his crew's reactions to all this. And as old fashioned as some might consider it, Kirk knew that peril was always more easily faced when standing shoulder to shoulder with one's comrades.

The thought occurred to him that there were those who might criticize this mass announcement as contrived dramatics. To blistering hell with any such critic! He damn well intended to use anything and everything that would help weld these people together into the crew that he was going to need.

It was 0404 hours when Kirk entered the great multilevel Rec Deck, the largest single interior ever designed into a starship. The four hundred plus crew members had gathered in loose ranks across the vast deck area, spilling onto upper balconies and against the huge observation ports which looked out into the orbital dry dock, busy with last minute launch preparation.

This Rec Deck interior was three, perhaps four times the size of Enterprise's former recreation area, before the redesign – and this without including the exercise rooms and sports areas adjoining it. There were many (none of them deep space veterans) who thought this new design a wasteful preoccupation with games and sociability. But those whose space experience was numbered in years knew that the function served here was as necessary to a starship as its engines. Here the most vital of the ship's mechanisms were kept in peak operating efficiency through music, song, games, debate, exercise, competition, friendship, romance, sex – the list was as endless as human ingenuity itself. Companionship and community were as basic to life support as oxygen and food. To those who might spend years of their life in this vessel, this place was their village square, their park, library, café, family table, their mall, meeting hall, and much more.

The sounds of chatter and shuffling feet died away as Kirk entered and crossed to the platform facing them. At his signal, Uhura switched the main Rec viewer to the recording of the Epsilon subspace transmission. There was the expected reaction to the K't'inga class heavy cruisers, the puzzled wonderment over the luminescent 'cloud'. Kirk was surprised to find his attention wandering as if these images were some fictional adventure he had seen once too often. But his attention returned, and with full intensity, as the first green whiplash energy bolt struck spectacularly and the first Klingon cruiser imploded into nothingness.

When it was over, Kirk looked out at all the faces he knew and the many he didn't, seeing that many of the new ones seemed almost impossibly young. He knew that most of them were wondering if they had just watched their own deaths on the viewer here. He could also sense that he had been right to change uniforms and wear Captain's stripes once again.

'That's all we know about it, except that it is headed for Earth. Enterprise is the only starship within interception range.'

There was a stir, and a few murmurs at that. He continued: 'Our orders are to intercept, investigate, and take whatever action is necessary and possible. We assume there is a vessel at the heart of the "cloud". It is our hope that there are life forms aboard that vessel which reason as we do.'

Kirk had intended for it to end with that. He knew that what they had just seen might panic a few members of the crew – some might even request relief from this assignment – he had already given orders that an immediate non-prejudicial transfer out should be granted in any such case. He turned toward the crew intending to dismiss them.

'Captain, we have an urgent subspace call from Epsilon Nine.' It was Uhura, referring to the outpost station whose sensor drones had gathered the Klingon destruction images which they had just seen.

'Put in on the viewer here,' said Kirk. From now on, the crew deserved to have as much information on the Intruder as he could provide to them. He saw Uhura keying the viewer to pick up the incoming subspace message – the usual flutter of hyper-dimension static, then the huge viewer settled into an image of Lieutenant Commander Branch, who commanded this outpost station near the Klingon border. He was flanked by a sensor operator and a pretty, young female lieutenant on scanner duty.

Kirk got a nod from Uhura, then called: 'Hello, Branch, this is Kirk, Enterprise. What do you have for us?'

The viewer image now showed more of the outpost, its array of powerful sensors and long-distance tracking equipment, and out an observation port through which faint starlight revealed the vast complex of antennae which stretched out into cold space in all directions around the central core of the outpost.

'The Intruder is holding its Earth heading,' Branch

was saying, 'and is now passing our station within visual range of us. We can give you a fairly close look at it if you'd like.'

The outpost's main observation port came into prominent focus on the Enterprise viewer and Kirk could see the strange 'cloud' much closer now than ever before. What had been a strange luminscence in longer views of it could now be seen to be made up of bizarre patterns of glowing colors which combined into great geometrical displays.

Branch checked console readings, spoke to the viewer: 'Enterprise . . . what we're seeing there is definitely a powerfield of some kind. Measures . . . over eighty-two A.U.'s in diameter. Must be something incredible inside there generating it.'

Eighty-two times the distance from Earth to the sun?

But Branch was looking up from the console, gravely. 'We're transmitting linguacode friendship messages on all frequencies. No response.'

'I have a null reading at the center of the cloud, sir,' the technician said.

'Definitely something inside there,' the pretty lieutenant added, 'but all scans are being reflected back. Receiving an odd pattern now . . . they seem to be reacting to our scans.'

'Some kind of energy surge,' Commander Branch said, looking up. 'Enterprise, they could be mistaking our scans as a hostile act.'

Kirk saw Branch stiffen at a reading – he knew the look.

'*Deflectors, emergency full!*' Branch hit an alarm button. The alarm Klaxon sounded. The viewer image distorted, wavered, cleared again – Branch reacting to it: 'We are under attack!'

'External view,' Kirk snapped. Uhura keyed a switch getting an outside view of the outpost as a pinpoint of writhing green fury could be seen emerging from the cloud – it was identical to the whiplash bolts which had destroyed the Klingons. Groans came from out among the crew assembled there. It was no recording they were seeing – this was happening *now* and it was frighteningly real. Then someone screamed.

There was simply nothing anyone could do – here or out at the distant outpost. The writhing fury struck outpost Epsilon Nine with cataclysmic force and as the viewer image broke up, the Starfleet outpost had already become a maelstrom of flaring energy and shattered debris. Then there was nothing.

'Viewer off.' Kirk said it quietly. It took effort to turn back to the assembled crew and face them again. Was there anything he could say to them now? No, he decided. For those who could not handle what they had just seen, nothing he could say could change how they felt.

'Pre-launch countdown,' he said, 'will start in forty minutes. Dismiss.'

CHAPTER NINE

The sight of the destruction of outpost Epsilon Nine had cost Kirk thirty-one of his crew sent back to Starfleet. It was less than he had feared, and only half of those had actually requested reassignment. The rest probably could have been kept on had there been no replacements available. Fortunately, despite the rumors of 'suicide mission', there were still hardy types down in Starfleet who could not resist challenge.

Countdown was now frozen at launch minus twenty-one minutes, holding there while replacements and a few late crew arrivals were being beamed up. The transporters were working perfectly now and even Kirk was satisfied that the problem had been solved. Meanwhile, he had done his best to gather up all those tenuous and undefinable 'reins of command' by which a starship becomes a community, then a family. It was sometimes as small a thing as a remembered name or a familiar old joke. For the moment, he was happy to take advantage of his 'living legend' reputation. Although created by Nogura for other purposes, it was undeniably useful in attracting loyalty among the new faces here. His old crew would ignore it, of course – they supported him for their own reasons – and the balance of the ship's complement were accepting, so far, the near-impossible demands he was making upon everyone.

The turbolift deposited him on the bridge.

In all these hours since the center seat had been his, he had not actually found time to sit in it. He stepped down into the helm area, unaware of the curious glances from some of the bridge crew. Uhura was there, and Sulu. It seemed strange to see Chekov at the newly designed weapons-defense console, but he was delighted that the young Russian held this important shipboard post, particularly now. He noted that despite the young lieutenant's boyish look, he carried himself with self-confidence and authority, a fully grown man.

Kirk touched the strange newness of the center seat, looked approvingly at the new emergency motion-restraints which were fitted there as well as at all other bridge positions. Sensor controlled, they would hold him firmly in the seat despite any emergency which might override the ship's inertia dampening system.

Just how the hell do you get into the seat?

The restraints were made to close over his lap. Unfortunately, they were in 'closed' positions, effectively barring him from sitting in the seat. *Where was the switch? Was anyone watching? The Captain can't figure out how to work his own high chair?!*

Uhura was turning his way with a questioning look when his eyes lit on what he hoped was the control. Sulu had turned, too, as Kirk touched the switch. Fortunately, it worked. He sat down relieved. Was there a hint of amused comprehension on Uhura's fine-boned Bantu face? Sulu also gave him a small smile and nod.

'Never hoped to see you sitting there again, sir,' Sulu said. The grin made it clear that this very scrutable Asian helmsman was pleased to see Kirk back in the center seat.

'Countdown now at minus twenty-one minutes and holding, sir.' Kirk looked up to find Decker standing properly there at his elbow, apparently ready to supply any information which the captain required. He was handing over a status report on one of the new wafer-thin display boards. Kirk took it, relieved to see that the readout displays there were a familiar and comprehensible design.

Decker made his verbal report. 'Status report, Captain. Main systems can be counted on for only forty percent of rated capacity or less at this time. Auxiliary systems can deliver fifty to seventy percent. Weapons and warp drive have never been tested under operational conditions. Mister Scott believes he can deliver up to eighty percent of impulse power.'

'Warp engines?' asked Kirk.

'In my opinion they could be trouble, sir,' said Decker. 'They should have had weeks of simulator runs for proper balancing of anti-matter mix on this new design . . .'

'I'm aware of that, Mister Decker. Thank you.'

So far, so good. Kirk's scan of the status board seemed to indicate that Decker was performing the functions of an Exec properly, managing the routine of the vessel so that Kirk would be free to concentrate on command considerations. But when the additional pressures of Decker's science officer duties began to intrude on this . . .?

Uhura was taking a signal. 'Transporter room and Chief Engineer Scott report transporter system fully repaired and now functioning normally, sir.'

'Dock signals clear, sir,' Sulu added from the helm.

'Captain,' Uhura continued, 'transporter personnel report the Navigator, Lieutenant Junior Grade Ilia, is already aboard and en route to the bridge.'

Kirk happened to be looking at Decker and saw him react, startled.

'She's a Deltan,' Uhura added, the faintest weighted emphasis in her tone.

'And there are no finer navigators in Starfleet, Commander.' Kirk realized there was a suggestion of reproof in his voice and immediately regretted it. Uhura was the last one who needed instruction in diversity from him. She had probably been trying to warn him – and the other males on the bridge, too – that a Deltan female was about to enter their professional life. And Deltans being Deltans, a warning would be helpful to humans who knew what it meant.

Kirk had noticed that Decker seemed unusually tense since hearing Uhura's announcement. Chekov merely looked up for an instant with an expression of 'give me strength'. Only Sulu did not react, apparently attaching no special significance to Uhura's comment. But then, Deltans were an old and very highly evolved race, with so few of them serving in Starfleet that the helmsman could easily have never met one.

Kirk considered giving some additional explanation to Sulu – after all, he would be working in close proximity with her. But it was probably better that Sulu learn his own way and handle it on his own terms. Kirk knew that the compelling attraction which Deltans exercised on anyone of the opposite sex went further than mere physical appearance; it was, literally, *chemistry*. Subliminal scents called *pheromones* were released by both Deltan males and females, triggering hormonal responses in most humanoid life forms of the opposite sex. It was especially troubling to humans since the scents were outside their normal olfactory range – just as a dog whistle is outside human hearing range. But the effect of these Deltan *pheromones* were still felt by them, and an unsuspecting human was likely to find himself in considerable sexual excitement without understanding why. It could be troublesome aboard a vessel but it was usually worth it since Deltans were superb navigators.

Then the elevator doors parted – and revealed Lieutenant Ilia. Her aura of sensuality surprised even Kirk, even though he had been warned and had prepared himself for it. She somehow *felt* naked to him, despite her completely correct starship's lieutenant's uniform. Then he realized that the feeling of nudity came from the fact that she was totally hairless. So far as Kirk could tell, the only exceptions to this were her dark, delicate eyebrows and eyelashes.

She strode purposefully toward Kirk. 'Lieutenant Ilia reporting for duty, sir.' She pronounced it Eye-lee-ah, her voice carrying a suggestion of alien music. Kirk concentrated on handling it with suitable formality – he could feel the *pheromones* working on him, and he decided not to rise. He was, after all, the ship's captain.

'Welcome aboard, Lieutenant.'

Then he saw her eyes find Decker and lock on his. They shared a moment of unquestioned recognition.

'Hello, Ilia,' Decker said.

'Decker!' she said.

Kirk found himself eyeing the exchange with some concern. It was becoming clear that the two knew each other well, probably romantically. With anyone but a Deltan, of course, it would have been Decker's affair, no concern of Kirk's. But the fact she was a Deltan changed that. Still, he realized that if it had been a romance, they could not have fully consummated it or Decker would not be here. On the other hand if Decker was still attracted to her that could be a serious problem. Kirk

70

could hardly afford any risk to the man who was both his exec and science officer.

Decker turned toward the center seat, perfectly aware of what he knew Kirk must be thinking. 'I was stationed on the lieutenant's home planet some years ago,' he said.

Ilia was looking puzzled over Decker's sleeve stripes. She knew him to be a *captain*, posted to starship command. '*Commander* Decker?' she asked.

'Our exec and science officer,' said Kirk, his tone just formal enough to caution her against pursuing this subject.

'Captain Kirk,' Decker said, 'has the utmost confidence in me.'

'And in you, too, Lieutenant,' Kirk said pointedly to Ilia. He was immediately sorry that he had said it, but Decker's remark had irritated him and he had clumsily put his concern into words.

'My oath of celibacy is on record, Captain.' Ilia kept her tone respectful. 'May I assume my duties now?'

'By all means,' Kirk nodded. He was sorry her oath of celibacy had come up this way but it was a Starfleet requirement wherever Deltans served with human crews.

'Sir, Starfleet reports our last six crew members ready to beam up,' interrupted Chekov. 'But one of them is refusing to step onto Starfleet's transporter platform.'

At first Kirk thought of the transporter accident, then he realized what it really meant. For the first time since coming aboard, a smile came naturally to his lips. 'Oh? *I'll* take care of that.'

As Kirk hurried from the bridge, Decker took the conn. He was shaken by Ilia's presence. In the end it had come down to a choice of her or Starfleet and a starship command. He had chosen the starship; now he had lost that, too. He turned away abruptly. 'Mister Sulu, take Lieutenant Ilia in hand.'

Sulu's eyes popped. 'Sir?!' Then he understood. 'Yes, of course.' Sulu was puzzled by the strange feeling which had plagued him ever since the Deltan woman stepped onto the bridge. He turned to Ilia wishing he had been given time for a cold shower first. 'Your pre-programming is already set in, Lieutenant.'

Sulu felt it hardly prudent to stand up at this moment. But unlike Kirk, he had no choice and therefore tried to seem to be bowing to her as he rose – and then tripped and decided to pretend to be actually offering Ilia his hand. Then he immediately thought better of this, withdrew his hand abruptly and quickly employed it in very busily punching out equations on her navigator's console. 'It's all in the computer,' he mumbled, 'you'll have no problems . . .'

'*She won't, but you will, Mister Sulu*, thought Decker. But fortunately for all of them, the effect would lessen considerably as Ilia became accustomed to these surroundings. Her secreting *pheromones* now was merely an automatic reaction to the presence of unfamiliar males. Sulu was acting about the same way that Decker had reacted when he first encountered Ilia.

At this juncture, Sulu hit a wrong switch, triggering a beep which sounded at him accusingly while he fumbled to shut it off.

Ilia smiled sympathetically. 'I'm *sworn* to celibacy, Mister Sulu. That makes me as safe as any human female.'

That, thought Decker, was polite Starfleet fiction. The oath made her presence tolerable, but never entirely safe. But he owed it to her to apologize for what Kirk had said earlier. 'I know the Captain meant no personal insult,' he said to her.

Ilia kept her eyes on the console. 'I would never take advantage of a sexually immature species,' she replied. Then she looked up at Decker. 'You can assure him that's true, can't you?'

Decker felt the slow flush rising past his collar.

Kirk entered the transporter room to see Chief Janice Rand and her assistant bringing up the last five arrivals. He was pleased to see that although the expression of his former yeoman carried some tenseness from the horror she had undergone here, she was handling the transporter console, and herself, with cool, easy skill. He had always liked Rand.

As she gave Kirk a quick look, the five recent arrivals began leaving the transporter chamber. Kirk called through the intercom, 'What was the problem down there?'

'It was a commander who insisted we go first, sir,' a young woman answered. 'Said something about first seeing how it scrambled *our* molecules.'

Kirk was smiling inwardly as he turned to the comcon transceiver. 'Starfleet, this is Captain Kirk. That officer is to be beamed up immediately.' It took somewhat longer than 'immediately' but finally the transporter began to hum, the pattern shimmer appeared and began materializing into a familiar shape.

On the transporter platform, Dr Leonard McCoy looked himself over carefully, showing considerable relief at finding himself in one piece. He was heavily bearded and wore workshirt and pants, heavy boots, all of which fitted Kirk's information that McCoy had become something of a recluse while he researched application of Fabrini medicine among surface dwellers. He did not at all look like the chief surgeon of a starship. But the stance was still the same, the skeptical, protesting, down-home manner of the man who did not care to be caught being at home in the stars.

'Well, for a man who *swore* he'd never return to Starfleet . . .' Kirk began, letting a grin surface.

McCoy interrupted. 'What happened, Captain, sir, was that your revered Admiral Nogura invoked a little known, seldom used, reserve activation clause . . .'

Kirk listened less to the words than to McCoy's tone. Was it merely grumble? No, there was a snap to it that indicated some genuine anger. Apparently Bones had found pleasure in the way he was living now and he resented being yanked unceremoniously away from it.

'In simpler language, Captain, sir, they *drafted* me!'

'They *didn't*!' Kirk said it straight-faced but McCoy was immediately suspicious.

McCoy flared back angrily. 'This was *your* idea. It *was* your idea, wasn't it!'

The time was long past when me could be forced to serve on naval vessels. Nogura's 'drafting' of McCoy (at Kirk's request) had little more authority than moral persuasion. But McCoy had at least come this far, perhaps only out of curiosity, and Kirk did not intend to lose him now. He had too many questions about himself. *What was different about himself now? Had those three years down there done something to him?* McCoy would find the answer if anyone could. *Ship's Doctor* was a deceptive title since it described what was actually the most powerful man aboard the starship next to the Captain. Under certain conditions and circumstances, a ship's doctor could relieve even a starship captain from duty. Ship's Doctors like McCoy were especially important on long missions where a captain's power and freedom of action were so absolute that it could feel almost godlike – and delusions of godhood were not unknown in the center seat. Kirk had always been grateful for the system that put men like McCoy between himself and that kind of insanity.

'Bones,' Kirk began gently, firmly, 'there's a "thing" out there—'

'Why is any object we don't understand called a "thing"?' McCoy snapped.

'—headed this way,' Kirk continued. 'I need you.' Kirk offered his hand. It was ignored.

'Were you behind this?' McCoy persisted.

'I was. I need you, badly.'

'I thought you were.'

McCoy's blue eyes met his. It seemed a painfully long moment before McCoy reached out and took the proffered hand. And once done, it became the long hand clasp of two very old and very close friends reunited.

McCoy turned to Rand. 'Permission to come aboard?'

Rand grinned at him, elated. 'Permission granted, sir!'

McCoy was already moving toward the door, the grumbling beginning again as if needing to prepare himself for the worst. 'I hear Chapel's an M.D. now. I need a top nurse, not a doctor who'll argue every diagnosis. And . . .'

He moved on through the doors, his words trailing behind him.

'. . . they've probably redesigned sickbay, too. Engineers love to change things . . .'

But McCoy would probably have a field day with the

new life-science equipment – much of which had been built to his designs.

Meanwhile, Rand had checked her listing and was now calling to Kirk. 'No one else listed as coming board, Captain.'

Kirk gave her a nod and turned to the intercom. 'All decks, this is the Captain speaking. Prepare for immediate departure.'

CHAPTER TEN

Captain's log, U.S.S. Enterprise, stardate 7412.3. Per Admiralty orders included herein, Enterprise is now ready to depart orbital dock on my command. This is being accomplished approximately one hour ahead of the revised emergency schedule, and appended to this log are appropriate commendations listing exceptional efforts by both Enterprise and dockyard personnel. Also per Admiralty orders, I, James T. Kirk, do now accept and take operational command of this vessel.

Kirk eased himself down into the center seat. This place was officially his now and he let himself savor the first moment, pretending to survey the bridge stations. Not that he expected anyone to be deceived – but he knew they would be tolerant of a moment like this. His eyes fell on Decker, whose eyes were fixed rigidly ahead, his expression taut. Kirk felt sympathy, then reminded himself that if they survived, Decker would still have his own moment like this. But for James Tiberius Kirk to sit here again was like Lazarus stepping out into the sunlight.

'Dockyard ready on main umbilical,' reported Uhura.

Kirk nodded. 'Disengage main umbilical.'

The order was relayed and on the main viewer they could see the dry dock's great thick cord of feedlines and powerlines begin to detach itself from the vessel, floating away weightless. At the helm, Sulu's hand was edging toward the maneuvering thrusters, ready for the captain's next order.

Kirk waited for the 'all-clear'. Had he pushed too

hard? Decker had urgently recommended another three hours before departure. Although, undeniably, Decker knew the ship best, Kirk was certain that to launch late was to lose the momentum they had built up. A launch on a note of failure to meet one deadline would breed doubt about their ability to meet other deadlines still ahead of them. He had decided to go.

'Dock control reports ready, sir,' Uhura said.

'Helm ready, sir,' Sulu said.

'Orbital departure on plot, sir.' It was a new voice but yet it seemed to carry some understanding of what this moment meant to him. It was the Deltan navigator, Ilia.

'Yard command signalling, sir,' Uhura said.

'I have *go* on all stations here, Captain.' It was Decker who had made his final check and was confirming the starship's readiness.

'Maneuvering thrusters, Mister Sulu,' said Kirk.

'Maneuvering thrusters, sir.'

As Sulu's hand moved, Kirk knew that tiny jets of blue flame were briefly visible out there to dockyard workers. He watched the viewer intently, waiting to see the almost imperceptible rocking, drifting movements which would indicate that the dry dock tractor beams had released . . . *Yes, they've released us! She's floating free!*

'Hold station,' he ordered.

'Thrusters at station keeping, sir.'

She was under Sulu's control now and his experienced hands were holding Enterprise exactly at dry dock center. Sulu gave Kirk a nod that this control system, at least, was working perfectly. Kirk nodded.

'Maneuvering thrusters ahead, Mister Sulu. Take us out.'

Sulu's right hand played the thruster controls and

Enterprise began to move slowly forward – on the viewer they could see the dry dock girders beginning to slide slowly past them.

Outside they were watched by tiny human figures in workpods and others in spacesuits along the girders. Some of the dry dock technicians waved, others merely watched with what seemed weary satisfaction. No, the others were waving too. It would have been hard to be out there and not be moved by the sight of Enterprise emerging majestically from her orbital chrysalis.

Earth was a gigantic darkening shape, dominating the full half of the sky above them – the sun was just now completely disappearing behind the planet and a last atmosphere-flare of sunlight reflected for an instant against the white-blue of the starship's titanium exterior.

Kirk did not need to be outside to know the look of her departure. He had felt the grace with which she had let the delicate lacework of the dry dock slip from her shoulders, and now he could feel the clean freedom of space cooling her skin.

Something drew Decker's eyes toward the man in the center seat. Kirk's face wore a transfixed look, a communion with things in the realm of poetry, religion, passion . . . and much else that Decker understood too. He was surprised to find himself much less bitter than expected.

Although he had never served aboard a vessel with Kirk, he had wanted it badly enough as a young officer. Not even the memory of his own famous father, Commodore Matt Decker, could change the fact that Kirk was likely the finest ship commander in Starfleet's history.

At least, he *had been* the finest. Despite everything, Decker found himself hoping that it was still true.

Scott had long ago let the sounds of the engine room drift out of his conscious mind. He would have found it hard to explain how this left the sound of music there – he only knew that he now heard it again. Scott made another scan of the impulse engine board. Kirk would order power from there soon. The chief engineer's ship status viewers showed that the maneuvering thrusters had taken Enterprise well clear of the orbital dry dock now.

Scott could see a familiar flicker of power barely visible in the great intermix chamber – he was also aware of a low, throbbing sound like tightly-leashed thunder. At this power setting, only microscopic amounts of anti-matter and matter were entering the intermix chamber, but the annihilation of even a pinhead of matter was sufficient for the impulse power which the captain would soon request – and which Scotty would grant. Even this barest of intermix setting would thrust the Enterprise forward as though a thousand of the old hydrogen-fed rockets had been fired in unison up there.

Decker's intercom voice: 'Status, Engineer?'

'Intermix reads "go". Impulse power at your discretion, bridge.'

On his status viewers, Scott could see Sulu shutting down maneuvering thrusters. And then he heard Kirk's voice order to the helm:

'Impulse power, Mister Sulu,' it said. 'Ahead warp point five.'

At the trailing edge of the Enterprise saucer section, the two great impulse power throats suddenly glared star-white. Scott's thousand hydrogen-fed rockets would not have come near the explosion of power really happening there. No murmur of it could be heard inside the starship; her inertia-dampeners also kept the explosive acceleration from being noticed, except on the bridge readouts.

'Departure angle on viewer,' ordered Kirk. He intended to miss no part of this.

Behind them, a breathtaking panorama of the old orbital dockyard of San Francisco – but that installation was rapidly receding in size now and Earth's huge dark sphere began to dominate the center image as it showed a last sliver of atmosphere halo from the now hidden sun. Then, Earth itself began growing smaller, and then more rapidly smaller as the starship continued its acceleration. A grin from Chekov triggered similar expressions from Uhura and Sulu. Kirk was glad that they felt the full excitement of this too – and then he was jolted by the realization that their pleasure was closely connected with his presence here. It made him feel uneasy as he remembered how many planet departures he had shared with them and how little he had thought of that or of them during these past years. He wondered *why*? But he found it difficult to be philosophical and ecstatic at the same time.

'Viewer ahead,' he said.

The viewer shifted to show the star-spattered space ahead. Kirk let his eyes search for familiar patterns as he relaxed back into the command seat. Yes, it had begun right. He need have no fear of anything now . . . except losing this.

CHAPTER ELEVEN

McCoy came into sickbay without a word, his beard scratching Chapel's face during the one hug he gave her before he began to swear quietly at the look of the new medical equipment there. He expressed his unhappiness in enough detail for the tall, handsome woman to recover from the surprise of his entrance – and now she was able to sit back and watch with some amusement as he began a tentative and suspicious inspection of the gleaming array of highly sophisticated life sciences equipment.

Christine Chapel, M.D., had been a Ph.D. in biomedical research when she had volunteered seven years ago to serve on the Enterprise as its head nurse. During those years, her admiration for McCoy's medical ability had reached near to professional worship. She had learned more from him than from her more formal study and recent internship which had added M.D. to her titles. She knew that McCoy was undoubtedly secretly pleased over the high quality of the medical equipment here, although he would probably go on forever pretending that all he really ever needed was a patient in need and his own senses to guide him in seeking the truth of that patient's condition.

McCoy's other dictum was that the human body and mind contained physical protection and repair mechanisms of such efficiency and effectiveness that the primary and most proper function of the physician was to assist patients in healing themselves. She had seen enough examples of his incredible abilities in holistic medicine to know that most of his contempt for drugs and surgery was genuine. Yet, when the need arose, McCoy could be as skilled a surgeon as she had ever seen function and his pharmaceutical knowledge spanned half a hundred planets. And of the medical hardware here, most of it was the result of McCoy's own recommendations.

Despite more sounds of annoyance, McCoy could not take his eyes off the improved body-scan table with its remarkable capacity to render any part of a patient as transparent as if the body were constructed of layered glass. It was also capable of scanning a patient so thoroughly that it could measure even molecule pattern changes within a single cell of the body. Chapel could see he was also secretly pleased that Starfleet had provided Daystrom equipment which used some of the Fabrini medical symbols which McCoy had found and Spock had translated from the writings of a ten thousand year dead civilization.

'They tell me you've been certified a ship's doctor.' McCoy had turned now and was giving her a challenging look.

'Yes, Leonard. I was certified two years ago.' She saw a blink of surprise at her use of his first name. But her title and medical degrees were as legitimate as his – even though she had served him as a nurse during almost five years out there.

'Doesn't it bother you that I'm taking over?' challenged McCoy. 'You've just been demoted to *assistant* to the ship's doctor.'

'And I have never been so pleased and relieved over anything in my life.' Not even McCoy could doubt the look of sincerity in her blue eyes.

'Let me see your medical log on the Captain,' McCoy said.

Chapel almost sighed in relief. If McCoy were testing her, he would find her well prepared on this subject. During all those years of working with McCoy she had come to understand the importance of the relationship between a starship's captain and chief medical officer. At the heart of this relationship was the fact that a ship's doctor was charged with grave responsibilities concerning the captain's physical, emotional and mental health, plus the authority to relieve that ship's captain from duty under certain circumstances. It could not be otherwise in a service where exploration was reaching so far into the galaxy that a starship captain might go for a year or longer without any contact with the Admiralty.

McCoy sat studying Chapel's log entries, clearly impressed over the amount of information she had accumulated. She had been helped by the fact that the medical *perscan* device had become routine in starships – it was a tiny scanner-transceiver device which was now worn by all crew members, permitting the body's vital signs to be monitored from sickbay at any time. (In the new full dress and duty uniforms, it was part of the belt ornament, this center-abdomen position being the ideal location for a medical scanner.) This information, of course, was kept as confidential as all other medical records* but it did have the considerable advantage of providing the ship's medical department with a continu-

* The *perscan* transmits its readings code-scrambled and directly into the medical computer where a previously authorized voice-print is necessary for any unscrambled read-out. Any such data concerning the ship's captain can be obtained *only* by the ship's doctor.

ous, all-conditions physical status report on everyone aboard the starship.

'These anagram conversions on the Captain mean what?' asked McCoy. 'Do you see them as stress indications?'

'Definitely. Don't you?' Her firm tone elicited a quick glance from McCoy; he could see that she was cautioning him that this represented no casual medical analysis of Kirk's present physical condition. Although it represented only fifteen hours of perscan records (since Kirk had arrived aboard), Chapel had also obtained other records on Kirk from Starfleet, and her comparisons of the two showed definite indications of recent strong emotional stresses of some sort.

McCoy had felt some vague worries about Jim Kirk from the moment he had heard his former captain had somehow regained command of the Enterprise again. After all, McCoy's resignation from the service had concerned this very subject. Upon learning that Admiral's stars were to be offered to Kirk, McCoy had protested vehemently and had secured the backing of other prominent medical officers in the fight. It was not that McCoy had any objection to his friend being promoted and honored – his was a medical protest over the fact that Kirk's psychological profiles were being ignored by the Admiralty in offering the promotion. When McCoy's protests were rejected by Nogura, *callously* rejected in McCoy's opinion, he had angrily resigned from Starfleet. McCoy had grown to know Kirk too well to have any hopes that he could adjust at this point in his life to an Earthbound existence – or for that matter to any existence that did not offer at least some of the challenges and freedoms which Kirk had known in starship command.

What was Chris Chapel saying . . .? It was something that paralleled his own thoughts, about Kirk.

'. . . and in his case,' Chapel continued, 'starship command fitted his psychological needs so perfectly that deprivation of it produced physical and emotional symptoms remarkably like those associated with narcotic withdrawal.'

McCoy looked up sharply, intending to comment that this was like comparing apples and coconuts. But the medical information being shown him by Chapel suggested that her analysis of Kirk's condition might be surprisingly close to the real truth.

Jupiter was coming up fast, massive, its colorflow patterns looking as artificial as always. Kirk had not been so close to this immense planet in eight years, and he marveled how the great red spot, with its dark center now larger than ever, seemed like a great eye looking out towards them. Several of Jupiter's moons were in view, Io and Ganymede particularly, reminding Kirk that the movement of these moons seen through Galileo's telescope had been one of humanity's first proofs that Earth was not the center of the universe. The so-called mutant-farm civilizations of pre-history had known this, of course, but their information had been a gift and not the result of human labor and growth.

'Jupiter comcon has been advised of our intended warp speed plot,' reported Decker.

Kirk nodded an acknowledgement. So far, Decker's performance of his exec and science officer duties had been more than satisfactory. Not that Kirk did not expect problems sooner or later, but meanwhile it was pleasant to sit and watch Jupiter slip past them.

In the last few centuries mankind had pyramided Galileo's discoveries into knowledge and feats which few early scientists could have ever imagined. Was it Einstein or Clarke who had foreseen the scattered necklace of energy collectors linking Sol and Earth? Kirk remembered reading of an O'Neill who had predicted the delightful range of planettes which humans had eventually constructed, the latest and largest of which had been made possible by the useful combinations of materials and chemicals abundant here in Jupiter's mini-solar system.

The moon Io had held some shocks for the first Earth scientists to land there, although not nearly as shattering as the discovery that Earth's own moon had once served as a base for space voyagers (their identity still a mystery) who had conducted genetic experiments with Earth's early life forms a million or more years before human history had begun.

Kirk saw the navigator Ilia press in the heading and course alternations he had requested earlier. He saw her look toward him and nodded his acknowledgement that her navigation plot was ready.

Captain's log, stardate 7412.6. Two point seven hours from launch. We have delayed engaging warp drive until now so that fuel balance simulation tests could be completed. Although both our Chief Engineer and Exec are unhappy with our test results, I cannot risk delaying any longer. We must intercept the Intruder at the earliest possible time.

Jupiter was behind them now, receding on the viewer. Kirk had sensed that Decker, at the science station behind him, had his computations ready but was not entirely happy with them.

'Captain,' said Decker as he continued to double check his console equations, 'assuming we have full warp capacity, accelerating to warp seven will bring us to I.P. with the Intruder in twenty point one hours.'

'Science Officer's computations confirmed,' said Ilia.

Kirk's peripheral vision caught an exchange of more than just a casual glance between the Deltan and his Exec and Science Officer combination. This was interrupted by the port elevator doors parting, revealing a clean-shaven and correctly uniformed Doctor McCoy coming onto the bridge. Good old Bones. Kirk could feel his spirits brightening further, despite the doctor's dour expression.

'Well, Bones, do the new medical facilities meet with your approval?'

'They do not,' McCoy stated emphatically. 'It's like working in a damned computer center.'

'Program now set for standard warp entry,' said Decker to Kirk.

Kirk started to turn to the helm, but Decker hadn't finished. 'Captain, this is your decision to make, of course, but I still recommend additional fuel simulation studies.'

'Mister Decker, the only point in intercepting the Intruder is to have time to investigate it before it reaches Earth. That means we need warp drive, *now*!' Kirk was aware that McCoy was giving him a curious look, but Decker's request for further fuel studies deserved a stern reply. Kirk hit the intercom switch. 'Engineering, stand by for warp drive.'

Scotty's worried reply came immediately. 'Captain, we need further warp simulation on the flow sensors . . .'

'Engineer,' Kirk persisted, 'we need warp speed now!'

'You're pushing, Jim,' said McCoy gently. 'Your people know their jobs.' Kirk found himself resenting the doctor's intrusion. *I know my job, too, Doctor*, said the look he gave McCoy.

'Hold on for one minute please, Captain,' Scott said. Kirk held. Through the intercom Kirk could also hear the growing rumble of the intermix chambers as Scott nursed the engines toward warp level power. Scott and an assistant could be heard muttering in the background. Kirk heard the assistant say, 'I can't estimate it any better.' Scott's words sounded grim. 'Aye, lad.' Then into the intercom: 'It's borderline on the simulator, Captain. I canna guarantee that she'll—'

Kirk cut him off. Couldn't anyone comprehend the urgent need for an early interception of whatever was out there? 'Warp drive, Mister Scott,' he said firmly. 'Ahead warp one, Mister Sulu.'

'Accelerating to warp one, sir.' As Sulu began moving the helm, Kirk could feel the slight reverb of increasing power.

Almost a century ago, the first successful quantum leap of a starship into warp drive made a hash of all those theories based on too narrow or unimaginative an interpretation of Einstein's work. That first starship and those aboard her did not become pure energy. What happened, of course, was that when that starship reached the threshold of light speed, it also reached that boundary between 'normal' space and hyperspace. That boundary was *time*, making it appear to those first hyperspace travelers that the universe around their starship had suddenly begun to shrink in size. Beginning with warp one and increasing geometrically, the higher the warp speed, the 'smaller' the universe and the closer together the points within it become.

Meanwhile, Sulu had continued his steady count. '. . . now at warp point seven . . . point eight . . . point nine . . .'

'I have a *time continuum* indication . . .!' It was Decker calling a warning that their boundary approach was uneven.

'Warp one, sir,' offered Sulu.

Kirk swung his seat around towards the science station. 'Mister Decker—' he began. He never finished the sentence in the pandemonium of alarm Klaxons, bells and cries that began. On the main viewer, the hyperspace spiraling of stars and fluid light suddenly narrowed into a vortex, as if a plug had been pulled and the universe was being sucked spiraling down a cosmic sink drain.

'Wormhole!' Kirk snapped to Sulu. *'Get us back on impulse power! Full reverse!'*

Klaxons continued blaring loudly while the viewer offered a window on the time-matter distortion which the Enterprise had created. Stars became strange elongated shapes as the Enterprise was drawn deeper and deeper into the hyperspace vortex. The ship was beginning to rock violently.

'Negative helm control, Captain!' shouted Sulu above the din. 'Going reverse on impulse power!'

'Subspace frequencies are jammed by wormhole effect!' shouted Uhura. Decker, consulting his science viewer, simultaneously yelled his findings: 'Negative control from inertial lag will continue twenty-two seconds before forward velocity slows to sublight speed!' From the

Deltan navigator: 'Unidentified small object has been pulled into the wormhole with us, Captain! Directly ahead!'

'*Forcefields up full! Put object on viewer!*' Kirk had to shout it to make his words intelligible. Time distortion was becoming noticeable, affecting everything they saw or heard. The main viewer was showing a tiny point of light directly ahead of them. The ship's computer droned on, 'Collision alert! Collision alert!'

'Manual override,' Kirk shouted towards Sulu.

'No manual response!' Sulu worked futilely at his console controls.

'Navigational deflectors coming up!' the Deltan said, then added with alarmed dismay, 'Navigational deflectors inoperative, Captain!'

From the science console, Decker reported: 'I believe it's an asteroid, Captain!' He touched a main viewer control and the image there jumped two magnifications ahead, revealing the object hurtling toward them. No longer a tiny point of light, it was now a distorted-looking, pitted chunk of space rock – an asteroid, its bulk looming larger and larger on the viewer as it tumbled in on collision course with the Enterprise!

CHAPTER TWELVE

The main viewer showed a mountain-sized nickel-iron asteroid cartwheeling directly toward them. Sulu had the viewer at maximum mag and the Deltan navigator next to him had it computed almost instantly.

'Im - im - pact - pact - in - in - twelve - twelve . . .' Ilia's voice showed the time-distortion that was affecting everything around them.

Kirk fought to make his brain decipher all this naturally. Ilia's words must have been 'Impact in twelve seconds.'

'*Stand by on phasers!*' Kirk's order was to Chekov who understood them at least enough to engage the *phasers ready* control. Then Kirk heard 'Be-be-lay-lay-that-that . . .' *What the hell?* Then he saw that it was Decker, racing toward Chekov's weapons defense station.

What was Decker shouting? *Belay that phaser order? Arm photon torpedoes?* Yes, that must be it – Decker was careening in to reach past Chekov, hitting the torpedo arming switch.

There was no time to unravel any more of it. Decker would not have countermanded Kirk's order without some good reason. Kirk's mind reeled; time felt askew. How many of those twelve seconds were left?

Chekov was clearly fighting time-distortion confusion too. He seemed to be saying, 'Photon torpedoes armed.'

'Fire torpedoes!' came Decker's order. Chekov clawed for the right buttons. 'Torpedoes . . . away!'

The starship spit out huge balls of light energy which

seemed to float too slowly. Sulu had the main viewer down to mag three, and the hurtling asteroid's ugly pitted face was filling the viewer again. They could not have been two whole seconds from impact when the compressed fury of a photon warhead finally reached the asteroid. It was as if a jeweler's chisel had shattered a flawed diamond — the large asteroid was instantly, explosively, a thousand nickel-iron fragments slamming into the starship's forward deflector shields. The smaller pieces not deflected became sparkles of red and then white flame as they were destroyed by friction against the vessel's forcefield screens. Then a final huge asteroid fragment hit very hard, jarring the whole vessel as if in one last try at its destruction.

'We're out of it.' It was a relieved shout from Chekov, his words undistorted now. At the same instant, Kirk had seen a change in the main viewer image. *The lovely star patterns of normal space.*

'Helm control restored, sir,' called Sulu.

'We are holding velocity constant at warp point eight,' reported Decker. Kirk let him continue the job of collecting a ship status report, relieved to hear him getting 'negative damage' assurance from Chekov.

Kirk realized that his own role during this had been unusually passive. He had made no objections when his phasers order to Chekov had been overridden. Why had Decker forced the use of photon torpedoes instead? Phasers could have been fired almost instantly. The fact that the photon torpedoes take much longer to arm had put them within a split-second of destruction. What was in Decker's mind anyway?

'No casualties reported, sir.' It was Chekov completing his ship status report to Decker.

'Wrong, Mister Chekov, there *are* casualties. *My wits!*'
This was from McCoy. 'As in "frightened-out-of!" ' The
doctor had no foolish notions about there being any
virtue in fearlessness.

Decker had turned to the intercom again, calling
Engineering. 'In just a second, Exec,' muttered Scott's
grim voice. 'We're picking up the pieces down here.'

Kirk became aware of receiving a puzzled glance from
Uhura. *Why? Was she still wondering why he had still made no
objections to the exec's having countermanded his order?* He
himself was surprised to find how much effort it took to
turn to the intercom.

'I'll want warp drive as soon as possible, Mister Scott.'

'Understood, Captain,' Scotty's voice answered. 'But
it was our anti-matter imbalance that created the wormhole in the first place. It will happen again if we don't
correct it.'

'Mister Scott, there is an Intruder out there which is
now less than *two days* from Earth. We've got to intercept
while it still *is* out there!'

Scotty's voice showed some annoyed strain now: 'Aye,
we *understand* that too, sir! We're doing our best.'

Kirk flipped off the intercom and rose from his seat to
face Decker. 'Mister Decker,' he said in a flat tone, 'I'd
like to see you in my quarters. You have the conn, Mister
Sulu.'

'Mind if I tag along?' asked McCoy. Kirk wished
McCoy would stay the hell out of this but saw no way to
deny his legitimate interest in any command dispute. He
nodded to McCoy and crossed to an elevator, followed
by a grim-faced Decker.

Kirk had already wondered if the rather plain beige

94

and rust decor of the captain's quarters had been Decker's choice. He intended to discard the tracked chair and worktable as soon as possible – they reminded him painfully of his Starfleet staff office arrangements. He noted that his original bunk here had been replaced with one nearly twice as wide. The narrow old bunk was one bit of nostalgia he did not at all mind losing, although he doubted he'd be making much use of that extra space on this mission, for sleep . . . or anything else.

When they entered the captain's quarters, McCoy had faded into the background. Now Decker stood facing Kirk, waiting, his face impassive, showing no indication of feeling either contrite or concerned. Kirk broke the silence.

'Explanation, Mister Decker. Why was my phaser order countermanded?'

Decker was annoyingly cool and polite. 'Sir, the Enterprise redesign increases phaser power by channeling it through the main engines. When they went into anti-matter imbalance, the phasers were automatically cut off.'

It was not what Kirk had expected. He felt surprised, then chagrined as he suddenly realized that Decker had been forced to do what he had done. 'Then you acted properly, of course.'

'Thank you, sir. I'm sorry if I embarrassed you,' said Decker.

Embarrassing? Of course it was embarrassing. Kirk remembered seeing the early specs on the phaser design change. He had protested strongly and then had savagely ridiculed a design engineer's reply that a starship would have no use for phaser batteries unless its warp engines were operating. He had let himself assume that Starfleet had listened to his experience and had accepted his recommendations on this. What had happened to his mind down there to make a foolish assumption like that?

'You saved the ship,' said Kirk. It was true; he had no choice but to acknowledge it.

'I'm aware of that, sir.' Decker was unruffled, cool.

Kirk flared. 'Stop competing with me, Decker!'

'Permission to speak freely, sir?'

'Granted,' Kirk said tightly.

'Sir, you haven't logged a single star hour in over two and half years. That – plus your unfamiliarity with the ship's redesign – in my opinion seriously jeopardizes our mission.'

Kirk found that it took more effort than usual to beat his anger down and maintain control. 'I trust you will . . . nursemaid me through these difficulties, Mister Decker?'

'Yes, sir, I'll do that.'

Kirk peered at his exec in some disbelief. Was Decker challenging him? If so, Kirk wasn't going to risk admitting that it bothered him. 'Then I won't keep you from your duties any longer, Commander,' he said.

As Decker turned and left, Kirk whirled on McCoy. '*Yes*, Doctor?' McCoy said nothing, waiting until Decker left the cabin and the door had closed behind him.

'He may not be wrong, Jim,' said McCoy.

'Get out of here, Bones,' said Kirk, and he meant it.

McCoy shook his head. 'As *ship's doctor*, I am now discussing the subject of command fitness.'

Kirk felt his expression harden. 'Make your point, Doctor.'

'The point, Captain, is that it's *you* who's competing. You pulled every string in the book short of blackmail to get the Enterprise. Maybe even *that*.' Even as he said it, McCoy's eyes were shrewdly measuring Kirk's reaction.

'Are you here to determine *how* I obtained my command, Doctor . . . or my fitness to continue in it?'

'I'll settle for an honest answer to . . . *why*?'

Kirk was puzzled. McCoy seemed intently serious, and yet the answer to his question was so elementary. Kirk started to explain: 'The Intruder . . .'

'. . . was a Heaven sent opportunity,' interrupted McCoy. 'And one you knew would never happen again. It could put you on a starship bridge again, and even more miraculous than that, it would be the Enterprise bridge . . .'

Kirk exploded with anger. 'McCoy, that is ridiculous nonsense! There was a job to do and Enterprise happened to be the one vessel available . . .'

'And when this mission is over, you have no intention of giving her back!'

Kirk felt like he was somehow in the midst of some time-distortion again. What was McCoy saying? If he was hearing this right, McCoy could be suggesting something more than unfitness.

'I intend to keep her?' Kirk said tightly. 'Is that what you're saying, Doctor?'

McCoy was nodding. 'And I can tell you exactly how you hope to keep her. Whether you're actually aware of it or not, Jim, you are gambling that the Intruder will make it possible somehow . . .'

Kirk heard himself interrupting – and felt the chill of what he believed to be cold anger. Had he just threatened to physically throw McCoy from his cabin? Yes, something ridiculous like that, but McCoy was nevertheless continuing.

'. . . and if the Intruder *is* that dangerous and *if* you win, there'll be enough gratitude for you to name what you want. And if you *die* in the attempt – incidentally taking all of us with you – so what the hell? You'd rather be dead than give this up again, wouldn't you, Jim?'

Kirk realized that the chill had been . . . *fear*. Not fear of the Intruder, or fear of failure, or even of losing his command. There was a *Kirk* of Starfleet oaths and solemnly accepted responsibility and of professional pride, who could not take lightly even the *possibility* that the ship's doctor could be right, especially on the subject of those mysterious reaches of subconscious and unconscious motivations understood so well and yet handled so skillfully in the past. In all the time he had known McCoy, he had completely ignored his advice only once . . . on that day he accepted his admiral's stars.

'Bones,' Kirk forced himself to nod, 'I've wanted this badly. You're saying it's gone far beyond that . . .'

'Jim, it is an obsession that can blind you to far more immediate and critical responsibilities. Your reaction to Decker is an example.'

Kirk stared at McCoy for a moment; the word *obsession* had felt like a raw nerve being touched. Did it explain that nagging feeling he had had that he was not handling things in quite the way he had at other times? Was he putting personal needs ahead of professional responsibility? If so, and if he could not change that immediately, he must now consider returning command to Decker.

Before Kirk could answer, he was interrupted by Uhura on the intercom. 'Signal from a Federation-registered long-range shuttle, sir. She wishes to come alongside and lock on.'

'For what purpose?' Kirk asked.

Chekov came in on the viewer. 'It is a courier, Captain. Grade One Priority. Non-belligerency confirmed.'

'Very well, Mister Chekov, see to it. Viewer off.'

He turned back to McCoy, eye-to-eye, the question of his fitness still hanging there between them. 'Your opinion has been noted, Doctor,' he said. 'Is there anything further?'

'I hope not,' McCoy replied.

Kirk turned, letting McCoy have the final word and keyed his intercom to Engineering.

'Mister Scott, once we do get to warp power, I want you to get me an alternate power circuit to the phasers which bypasses the engines. I don't care what it costs in power. We've had enough times with engines knocked out to know we can't have our phasers dependent on them.'

From the other end he heard: 'Aye, sir, and I believe if you'll ask Mister Decker about this . . .'

Kirk interrupted angrily: 'Mister Scott! I will discuss it with my exec if or when I believe it necessary to do so! Kirk, out!'

Kirk snapped off the intercom. It was Decker who had been in charge of the Enterprise and had let that redesign error get past him. Kirk would never have permitted it even if he had had to buck it all the way to the Federation Council. But then Decker had never commanded a heavy cruiser in deep space.

Decker had left Kirk's cabin, still angry. Kirk was not stupid, but he flat did not know this ship! Decker *did* know it – limitations and all; he had argued the phaser design modification up through Starfleet's design bureau.

99

Finally, he and Scott had agreed that once they had her out of orbit, they would damn well rig a by-pass circuit. It was half-ready already, and once they had any spare time . . .

His thought was cut off as the turbolift opened in front of him, and Ilia stepped out. He stopped. It was no good. Not even his command crisis could block off this familiar old response to her presence. But he stood there trying to appear unmoved.

'Was he difficult?' Ilia asked, concerned.

Decker felt something giving way. 'No more than I expected.' He hesitated, then added, 'Not as difficult as seeing you has been. I'm sorry . . .'

'That you left, or that you didn't say goodbye?'

'If I'd seen you again, would *you* have been able to say it?'

She hesitated for a very long time, then shook her head. 'No.' She whirled and moved through her cabin entry, the doors snapped open and shut behind her, leaving him staring at it, remembering and regretful. Regretful? He had run like a thief. He regretted it had been necessary to run from her. But he had known that the Deltan unity through sex carried a powerful attraction for him, and that it might even shatter the fault-line of his own psyche. Decker was mostly what people took him for: Matt Decker's son. Solid, reliable, old-line Starfleet. But it was his mother who had raised the son while Matt Decker roamed the stars – and she had taken their son into the fringes of the *new human* movement, giving Will Decker a taste for the unusual reward potentials of unity.

Kirk took the conn, tried to focus his thoughts onto the courier vessel's arrival. McCoy was right. Damn it, how he wanted this! And not just now, for this one time. Suppose the Intruder changed course tomorrow? Or turned out to be something harmless to Earth? Would he be pleased, genuinely relieved and pleased if the danger was past? If not, he did not belong in this center seat. If he were to remain here . . . no, if he *belonged* sitting here, then the one and only function of his total being must be to this mission. He had no *right* to concern himself here with his own future, no more than one of his crew could be allowed to disobey one of his orders for some personal reason. The Starfleet oath was unyielding and plainly understandable on that point.

The craft now approaching Enterprise was, by official designation at least, a long-distance shuttle. But the term *shuttle* was one of those misnomers which are often perpetuated by tradition in a service like Starfleet. It had begun long ago with moon *shuttles*, which had led to larger planet *shuttles*, and now included this trim but powerful warp power craft which could have easily outraced the starships of only fifty years ago. It was, indeed, as foolish as calling the U.S.S. Enterprise a *heavy cruiser* which it was most definitely not. It was the most powerful Federation vessel in existence, deserving at least the old naval description of *battleship*, although some admiral or statesman in the distant past had apparently seen the term *cruiser* as more civilized and less militaristic. Actually, more proper and accurate of all would have been to term the Enterprise an *exploration and research vessel*, which best described its principal use and functions.

By whatever name, however, it was a sleek and lovely craft that was passing over Enterprise's bow, switching to impulse-retro power to wheel gracefully over, reversing its direction. It was skillfully done, the wheel-over no more than finished when the passenger cabin detached and began moving airlock first toward the starship's command airlock just a deck below the bridge. The craft's star-drive nacelle section continued to hover, waiting for the passenger section to discharge its passengers or cargo and then return and combine into the whole shuttlecraft again.

'Cabin now returning to shuttle,' announced Chekov's bridge relief. Whatever it had delivered to Enterprise, it had not remained attached to the starship for over a minute. The shuttle's cabin compartment could be seen again on the bridge viewer as it floated toward its star-drive reunion.

Decker came onto the bridge crossing to where Kirk was standing near the science console. As Kirk turned toward him, Decker was startled at what he saw in Kirk's face; there seemed to be a stranger looking out of Kirk's eyes. He had almost the look of *Nogura*!

'I want you to hear this, Mister Decker,' said Kirk touching the log button on the science console. 'Captain's log, supplemental. Note commendation for Mister Decker in that he took appropriate and proper action in countermanding my phaser order during the wormhole emergency. His knowledge and prompt action saved the ship. Kirk, out.'

'Thank you, Captain,' said Decker.

Kirk found himself liking Decker better for the fact that he had not said *I was just doing my job* or some nonsense like that. The commendation had been for doing that job *exceptionally well*.

At that moment the turbolift doors opened. The figure in the severe black robe was tall, striking. The deep set, almost burning eyes carried a vaguely satanic look.

It was Spock!

CHAPTER THIRTEEN

He had the look of fasting, of hot winds and blowing sands, and of difficult and painful disciplines mastered. He had the look of . . . *almost serenity*. It was of serenity so nearly achieved that it had left behind this dignity at least. Spock might have need of this dignity, for there was no serenity in his eyes.

Kirk seemed stunned. 'Spock . . .! Spock, *where? How* . . .?' Then there was a smile on Kirk's face, and he was moving to Spock with a hand outstretched.

But the Vulcan had turned, ignoring Kirk's presence, and was moving to the science console where Decker sat.

'Commander, if I may.' Spock's voice sounded unusually toneless. To Decker, it was and was not the Vulcan voice from the old Enterprise science tapes. But what surprised Decker most of all was this profound sense of awe felt at being in Spock's presence.

It took the Exec a moment to realize that Spock wanted to take over the science station position. He came hastily to his feet, trying to indicate yes, *certainly*! Decker knew without conceit that he was at least as good as any other human on this new console, but this was more like an amateur yielding a keyboard to an artist. Spock was sliding into the seat, intent on the computations he began keying into the maze of computer programming and retrieval systems.

Decker felt no disappointment over what he saw next. Spock's long fingers played over the closely packed banks of selectors, sequences and regulators with astonishing speed, each touch as deftly accomplished as if it had been done with painstaking concentration.

'I have been monitoring your Starfleet transmissions, Captain,' Spock said in that same dispassionate tone, 'and I am aware of your engine difficulties.' The considerable assortment of science console viewers were now displaying readouts whose rapidity began to lose and bewilder Decker – and then he was even more astonished as he remembered that Spock had never before sat at this particular console design, even though it reflected recommendations he had left behind in his science logs.

Spock paused, scanning the information displays on the console viewers. Then he turned to Kirk, still without any expression: 'I offer my services as science officer.'

Kirk's relief was absolute. If there was any way to get the starship into warp speed quickly, it had just somehow miraculously arrived. Kirk turned to Decker. 'If our executive officer has no objections—'

'Of course not,' Decker said quickly. 'I am well aware of Mister Spock's qualifications.' The young exec was close to forgetting the disappointment he had endured so far. How had Spock been conjured up at this very moment? Had this been arranged by Jim Kirk somehow? Decker found himself remembering again how those five years of Enterprise logs had been filled with instances of a Captain Kirk who seemed to keep achieving the impossible. Or if Spock had come here on his own, then at least it had to stem out of the well-known friendship between these two. And Spock's professional admiration for Kirk was equally well known. Either way, Decker's estimation of Kirk began slowly growing again toward what it had been in the past.

Chekov arrived back at his station, still looking stunned

over the surprise of having seen Spock step out of the shuttlecraft cabin. 'Mister Chekov,' Kirk said, 'record Mister Spock's Starfleet commission reactivated, and list him assigned as Enterprise science officer, both effective immediately.'

Although Kirk had been as dumbfounded as the others he was pleased to note that he had recovered first and was now handling all this with some degree of command presence. But it still felt painful to be reminded so powerfully and unexpectedly of his friendship and affection for Spock – theirs had been the touching of two minds which the old poets of Spock's home planet had proclaimed as superior even to the wild physical love which affected Vulcans every seventh year during *pon farr*. However, Spock's new demeanor warned Kirk to stay clear of personal considerations for the moment.

Spock came to his feet abruptly from the science console. 'The required fuel formula will need considerable cooperation from the chief engineer,' said Spock. 'I can go there immediately, unless the Captain wishes to question my tentative findings thus far . . .'

Kirk knew he was at last beginning to take firm command of this vessel and this mission – and this was as good a time as any to demonstrate that he was capable of dealing coolly and effectively with either good fortune or calamity, however unexpectedly one or the other might arrive.

'Just fix it, Spock,' said Kirk. 'Do it in any way that gets us to warp speed fastest!'

Giving no sign of acknowledgement, Spock turned to step toward the bridge turbolifts. At that moment, one of them now arrived, discharging Chapel and McCoy, out onto the bridge. It was plain that Spock intended to ignore them, too, just as he had the other familiar faces among the bridge crew – but they had moved in too quickly and were blocking his path.

As Chapel first saw him, black robed, almost regally Vulcan – she felt almost suffocating pain somewhere. And now she was standing in front of him, cursing herself for the fool she knew she must look as she tried to compose a simple sentence of greeting. She hated the silly smile she knew was brightening her whole face. 'Mister Spock . . .!!'

McCoy was almost as unsuccessful in hiding his own considerable pleasure. 'So help me, Spock, I'm almost pleased to see you.'

Spock's eyes had passed them rapidly, so totally devoid of interest that it seemed deliberate cruelty. Kirk came very near intervening, but held back, realizing that Spock could not be blamed for Chapel's fantasies concerning him. And McCoy was well able to look after himself.

'That's how we *all* feel, Mister . . .' This was from Uhura, who had hoped to convince Spock of the sincerity of everyone's welcome, but her words stopped as the same cold, uninterested glance passed her in mid-sentence.

Kirk could see a pattern emerging; except as duty situations required, Spock obviously intended to completely and impartially ignore every member of this starship's crew. The reasons for that might turn out to be as interesting as whatever it was that brought him here. Perhaps as painful, too. Kirk decided that it would not hurt Spock to be reminded that pain could be two–edged. He waited until the Vulcan was in mid-step into the waiting turbolift, then:

'Mister Spock! *Welcome aboard.*'

Spock hesitated for an instant – Kirk knew that his voice carried enough sincerity to call forth a memory or two in the Vulcan's mind. But although he had hesitated for an instant Spock continued on into the turbolift. He made no acknowledgement. The doors snapped closed and he was gone.

'Never look a gift Vulcan in the ears, Jim,' said McCoy. Kirk felt a grin beginning to form. It was a totally nonsensical statement that Bones had just made, but somehow Spock's very presence did seem to promise that everything was soon to get better.

CHAPTER FOURTEEN

'It should be possible to proceed without me now,' said Spock to the chief engineer.

'Aye, we can manage from here.' His Highland burr showed a twist of annoyance. 'But we'll miss the sound of your sweet laughter.' Spock ignored this as completely as he had the Engineer's outstretched hand two hours ago. Scott fought back an impulse to hurl some earthy obscenity after the departing Vulcan.

Damn Spock! Montgomery Scott was not accustomed to being ignored – especially not here in his own domain. *But what a fine engineer the Vulcan would have made. That should indeed have been his calling. No one expects pleasant temperament of an engineer!*

Accustomed as he was to Spock's powers of logic, Scott had been deeply impressed this time. After an hour at the engineering console, Spock shut down the computers which had been providing him with simulator formulas and engine data. Then the Vulcan had seemed to look into nothingness for a dozen long minutes. Finally, without a flicker of expression, he had proposed an intermix formula which computer-tests had shown to be within a hair of *perfect*! All that was left was to confirm it in the simulator runs which were under way.

Just past Scott's console, the great intermix chamber was showing the almost blinding flash patterns which meant that the engine anti-matter bleeders were beginning to work smoothly and properly.

Scott knew that this rumble of power could now be felt

on the bridge, too. His status monitors showed him that every division and department on the great starship was tightening down for another attempt into warp speed.

Spock made his way to the extreme forward area of the engineering hull. It was here that a labyrinth of forcefield generators and spider-webbed hull supports provided a maze of odd-shaped cubicles which some architect-pyschologist had designed into comfortable and private alcoves, each with its individual view of the stars. This was in some ways the most pleasant area of the starship, being as it was a casual design afterthought and without the purposeful efficiency of the rest of the vessel. It was popular as a place for the many pleasures which a crew member might find in solitude or in new friendships.

As he entered, Spock's ear caught the sounds of humans at love, which told him that privacy was still respected in this area of the ship. He moved quickly on, wishing his hearing was not so acute at times like this – it was the beginning of coupling he had heard and it distracted him. Odd, this human need to continually rub this and that part of their bodies together, particularly since humans conducted it while fully rational, sometimes even intermixing it with conversation, which was certainly far from any definition of *passion* by Vulcan standards.

He passed two hatches bearing the infinity symbol, which reserved them exclusively for meditation, but both were in use. Good. Even in this crisis, human frailty had to be kept in mind. Strange how the Earth species needed regular relief from even the mildest of stress situations – the result, of course, of the energy they continually and so foolishly wasted on emotional trivialities.

Excellent! Here, not in use, was an alcove with one of the wide, circular observation ports. He closed the hatch behind him, and in the darkness touched the control which spiraled open the protective iris of the circular port – it was like opening the pupil of a great eye onto the splendor of space. He kneeled Vulcan-fashion, composing his physical body so that he could exclude his six animal senses from his consciousness.

It helped to look out into the stars. It was satisfying to feel the vastness out there and to know that he was not only a small part of that, but the All of it, too. His *seventh* sense* had long ago assured him of this, just as it was doing again now, that this relationship of consciousness and universe was the only reality which actually existed. The Masters at Gol, of course, spent much of their lives seeking to unravel the puzzle of how a living consciousness could at every moment be both *part* and *All*. Spock tried to imagine some form of mathematics which might express this – and as hopeless as he knew it was to apply finite symbols to infinite puzzles, the exercise slowly cleared his mind, and his meditative state deepened.

Spock did not achieve the *Kohlinahr* level of meditation which he sought. He suspected that it was never to be his again. Had he achieved *Kohlinahr*, all remembrance of this life and these people would have become patterned logic without overtones of either pain or pleasure. Even

* To Vulcans, the sense of oneness with the All, i.e. the universe, the creative force, or what some humans might call God. Vulcans do not, however, see this as a *belief*, either religious or philosophical. They treat it as a simple fact which they insist is no more unusual or difficult to understand than the ability to hear or see. (The Vulcan *sixth* sense, referred to earlier, is merely the ability to sense the presence of or disturbance in magnetic fields – a sensory ability not uncommon among some Earth species as well.)

III

having failed in Gol, he had hoped that the long study and disciplines would at least extirpate the emotions this vessel and its humans had once evoked in him. It was not to be – on arriving here, the mere sight of the Enterprise had increased his heart rhythms noticeably. The other physiological changes which beset him on entering the bridge were so shocking that they made him scorn himself.

There was much to put out of his mind. Why was it difficult to forget Chekov's astonished delight which greeted him at the command airlock when he boarded? And on the bridge – *Kirk*! The mere name made Spock groan inwardly as he remembered what it had cost him to turn away from that welcome. *T'hy'la*! And there had been McCoy, so humanly human – and, yes, of course Chapel with her bizarre and impossible fantasies of one day pleasuring him. Sulu the romanticist, Uhura of the lovely star-songs . . .

Spock's mind opened. It was there! He waited.

Then, it touched his mind! The same awesome consciousness he had felt on Vulcan, and that had drawn him here! A cascade of patterns of logic almost geometrical in their breathtaking perfection!

He had no doubt now but that it issued from the strange cloud-like shape rushing toward Earth, and he tried quickly to analyze it. Was it one mind . . . or many minds all working in unity? He thought very probably the latter, since he could sense myriads of thoughts passing in overwhelming profusion and rapidity.

Then it was gone. Yet, this time Spock sensed some part of that *consciousness* lingering out on the fringes of his thoughts. Was it monitoring, waiting? Waiting for what?

Spock turned to his memory, forcing it to slowly, very slowly, replay this last encounter. *Yes! Spock was startled*

Captain James Kirk on the eve of his newest and most dangerous mission . . .

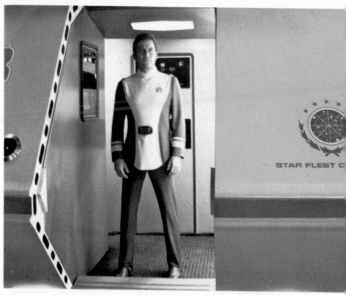

Captain Kirk approaches the nerve centre of Starfleet Headquarters

Malfunction in the starship's transporter room . . .

Commander Decker and Navigator Ilia

The crew of the refitted U.S.S. Enterprise

Commander Decker in a tense moment on the bridge of the U.S.S. Enterprise

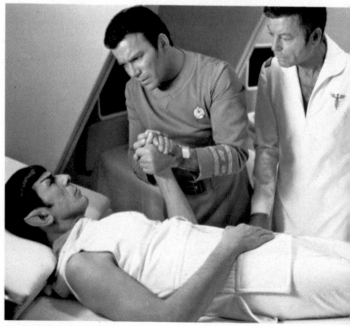

Mr Spock has returned . . .

. . to boldly tread once more towards the menace from
outer space

Security Officer Chekov samples the dangers that will
follow . . .

..... As Kirk, Spock and Dr McCoy confront the seemingly invincible destructive power that threatens the Earth — and the human adventure is just beginning.

with the sudden clarity of the answer — in all those tumults of thought and consciousness there had been a sense of puzzlement — and a strange hint of desperation in that puzzlement.

For a second time, he had sensed not only logic, but awesome knowledge. What was there that could still puzzle the knowledge and logic of that greatness? What was it so desperately seeking? Spock was certain that he had not erred in searching for his own answer here. Was it possible that this *immensity* could have some need which might be fulfilled by an insignificance called *Spock*?

CHAPTER FIFTEEN

Captain's log, stardate 74134. Thanks to Mister Spock's timely arrival – and assistance – engines are rebalanced to full warp capacity. Repair time less than three hours, which permits us now to intercept Intruder while still more than a day from Earth.

Kirk glanced toward the science station. Spock had returned there just moments ago, now in regulation uniform and haircut but still deep in the same self-isolation. Sulu was giving a curious glance in that direction, too. The helmsman had no doubt that Spock's presence increased their odds of survival. But he could not help thinking that the old Spock would have improved those odds even more.

'Ready, Captain,' said Scott's intercom voice.

'Stand by to give us warp power,' replied Kirk.

'Our engines are not yet perfectly balanced, Captain,' said Spock. 'But I have adjusted our intermix formula accordingly.'

Decker had come out of a turbolift during this, his eyes scanning bridge consoles as he moved to Kirk's side. 'Recommend yellow alert, all decks, Captain.'

'Quite unnecessary,' said Spock.

'Yellow alert, all decks,' ordered Kirk. He had gone with Decker's recommendation as much out of curiosity as anything else. But the Vulcan gave no indication that he had either heard or cared.

Meanwhile, Chekov had begun the alert; the Klaxon

was blaring. 'Yellow alert, all decks; yellow alert, all decks, yellow . . .' The computer voice stopped in mid-word as Kirk touched the silencer.

Decker was looking at Spock apologetically. 'I'm not questioning your computations, Mister Spock. But it *is* close to the same formula that put us into the wormhole last time.'

It annoyed Kirk to see how completely Spock was ignoring this. Considering what had happened on their last attempt, Decker was right in recommending everything be buttoned down.

'Science Officer,' said Kirk, 'I'll trouble you to acknowledge our Executive Officer when he speaks to you.'

Spock turned to Decker. 'There is not the slightest risk of a hyperspace rupture, Executive Officer.'

Kirk turned toward Sulu. 'Ahead to warp one.'

'Warp one, sir. Beginning acceleration.'

They could all feel the power throb, the primal fury of matter and anti-matter shattering into energy – then the surge forward which not even their inertial dampeners could quite handle. Despite the certainty in Spock's statement, an eddy of tension could be felt circling the bridge.

'Warp point nine . . . point nine two . . . point nine five . . . point nine eight . . .' Sulu's auxiliary viewers showed the power effect building between the great engine nacelles. Any instant now, either a smoothly accelerated entry into hyperspace, or . . .

The quantum shift happened; the star mass congealed in front of them in an eerie blaze of cold light.

'Warp one, sir.'

Kirk forced himself to wait out the long interval which

had passed last time before apparent success had dissolved into chaos.

'Cancel yellow alert,' he finally said to Chekov. Then to Sulu: 'Take her on up, helm.'

Everybody breathed and Kirk turned toward the science console where he would have liked to at least nod his gratitude, but Spock was immersed in calculations.

Scott's elated voice could be heard on the intercom. 'Proper treatment, that's all this lady wanted, Captain. She's not even strainin' now!'

They took her up by smooth, unfaltering stages to warp seven point six one. Spock had marked this as their limit until engines received a final balance. Then, when everything had been checked, Kirk rose, keying his intercom. 'Doctor McCoy, please meet me in the officer's lounge in five minutes.' He moved for the elevators, adding: 'I'd be obliged if you could join us there too, Mister Spock.'

The officers' lounge was located three decks below the bridge at the forward edge of the command superstructure. The observation ports here looked out over the starship's vast 'saucer' section and provided the best shipboard views of space and, at warp speeds, of hyperspace. With the ship in warp drive now, the myriads of stars visible from here were coalesced into a mass ahead of them – and the starship's incredible velocity was obvious even there as occasional stars would seem to abruptly slip free of the rest, whipping brightly past the starship to vanish into the reverse coalescence of stars behind them.

McCoy liked the officers' lounge. It pleased him that Starfleet could understand the necessity of providing luxury like this, especially for those whose years of service and distinction merited it. And it was made doubly pleasant by the fact that entry here was forbidden to no one – its exclusive use by command grade officers was merely a tradition which had grown out of the honest respect which Starfleet's senior officers had earned.

The Vulcan came in, still cold and aloof. 'Reporting as ordered, Captain.'

McCoy felt half-angry and half-pitying. Despite the cold Vulcan exterior being presented by Spock, McCoy had known him too well for too many years to miss the small signs of human torment that were present, too. It annoyed the doctor that Spock, so perfectly logical in other things, felt compelled to repudiate his human bloodline – it also troubled him that the strain of this might push Spock past some breaking point.

'Sit down please,' Kirk said.

Spock remained standing. 'Sir, I would appreciate Doctor McCoy absenting himself from this interview.'

McCoy saw Kirk's look harden. 'I want him here,' Kirk said. '*Sit down!*'

This was unmistakably given as an order – even then, for a moment, it looked as if Spock would refuse. Finally he sat, but formally, rigidly, his eyes centered on the Captain alone.

Kirk decided to maintain the official tone in his voice. 'Your arrival report stated that while on Vulcan you sensed unusually strong thought emanations which seemed to be part of some entity or entities traveling in this direction. Can you tell us any more about these thoughts?'

Spock answered equally formally. 'I could sense only what seemed an almost omniscient pattern of perfect logic, sir. I can explain nothing more; I understand nothing more.'

'Have you had any contact with this consciousness since then?' asked McCoy.

Spock kept his eyes on Kirk, presenting his answer there. 'Affirmative. Since arriving aboard, a second contact in which I sensed some puzzlement; also some urgency in needing some answer. As to the nature of the puzzle, I have no clue.'

'Is that all of it so far?' asked Kirk. 'Two mind contacts with something out here? Nothing more?'

Spock wished Kirk's question had not been asked so broadly. 'On Vulcan, I seemed for a moment to be also sensing *your* thoughts, Captain. It felt as if you were wondering whether the Klingon cruisers and crews were actually destroyed . . . or had been converted into exhibits of some sort.'

Kirk's expression told McCoy there had indeed been such a thought – although this surprised McCoy much less than the fact that Spock had admitted sensing it, considering his present unfriendliness. It was common knowledge that telepathic rapport between Vulcan and human was possible only in cases of extraordinarily close friendship.

Kirk nodded casually. 'I must have been wishing that I could discuss all this with you. I had acquired the habit of having you around during emergencies.'

McCoy watched as Spock continued to sit staring expressionlessly straight ahead. *Why couldn't Spock respond to him? Kirk could hardly risk begging one of his officers for friendship.*

'I heard you went to Gol after you left,' Kirk said. 'Were you studying with the Vulcan Masters?'

'That question invades my personal life, Captain.'

'Emotion, Spock?' McCoy had seen the barest flicker of expression at Kirk's mention of the Masters. 'Is it possible you failed?'

Spock turned slowly toward McCoy, acknowledging his presence for the first time. 'Your deductions do you credit, Doctor, if your puerile curiosity does not.'

'My *professional* curiosity, Science Officer.' McCoy was capable of a formally official tone, too. 'And am I seeing *anger* now?'

McCoy had seen a glint of it even though Spock had composed his expression almost instantly. It was precisely this kind of thing which had made Spock object to the doctor's presence here. He had no choice but to nod stiff acknowledgement of the truth of McCoy's observation, but he addressed himself back to Kirk.

'I had believed that a discipline at Gol would exorcise my human half. I did not succeed . . . I have not *yet* succeeded in fully accomplishing that.'

'The fact that you had sensed patterns of perfect logic,' Kirk had to ask. 'Does that have something to do with your being here?'

'It is my only hope of accomplishing what the Masters could not,' said Spock.

'Isn't it lucky we happened to be going your way,' said McCoy.

'Let it drop, Bones,' Kirk said. But he kept his tone firm as he continued, to Spock: 'You are my science officer – I'll expect an *immediate* report on anything further you learn or *sense* from here on.'

'I have accepted service here as a Starfleet officer,' said Spock, stiffly.

Kirk nodded, accepting the rebuke. 'This has been painful for me, too. Thank you.'

Spock turned and went out without a word. Kirk and McCoy exchanged a troubled look. Then Kirk turned to go, too.

'Jim . . .' called McCoy. Kirk turned back and McCoy waited until certain Spock was out of hearing range. 'However seriously Vulcans take their oaths, remember that everthing and everyone has a breaking point.'

Kirk shook his head. 'I can't believe Spock could ever be turned against us.'

'Jim, have you ever heard Spock exaggerate? If that *consciousness* is as enormous and powerful as he describes it, he may have no choice.'

Kirk came onto the bridge to find Spock already at his station, opaque and unreadable. Decker was in the command seat, which was perfectly proper, of course. The young Exec got up and came to give his report, handing over the display readout which showed present efficiency of Enterprise divisions and departments.

'Critical systems status improving markedly, sir,' Decker reported. He was pointing to Chekov's weapons and defense division which was now rated high – mid-eighties. Communications was equally high. Secondary and auxillary functions still showed marginal ratings but, of course, main effort and attention had been concentrated on their worst critical needs.

What was this? Decker's display board showed an interesting power bypass design . . . in fact, it was the very kind of thing Kirk had just mentioned to the chief engineer! This arrangement would permit the use of their ship's phasers even with all engine power knocked out.

'Something Scott and I had been putting together in our spare time, sir,' Decker said, with some satisfaction.

Kirk was genuinely surprised. According to the display here, a major part of this bypass arrangement had been installed. It said a great deal about Decker that he had not only been aware of this need but was also ingenious enough to have this much already accomplished. 'A pity there wasn't time to finish this,' Kirk said.

Decker grinned. 'Hoped you'd say that, sir. I think I've worked out a way to have these alterations completed and tested an hour before I.P. Permission to proceed?'

Kirk hesitated. It could be disastrous if some unforeseen problem occurred during further alterations — it could end with them drifting helplessly in the path of the Intruder with the work incomplete and *both* engines and phasers useless. Kirk resisted an impulse to ask him if he were certain of his estimates — Decker was as aware as anyone of their situation. And he knew this ship best. It was Kirk's moment to indicate how far he trusted his young second-in-command.

'Permission to proceed,' Kirk nodded. 'I'm very pleased and impressed with this, Will.'

'Thank you, sir.' Decker hurried toward the turbolift landing. Kirk took another look at the vessel and crew emergency breakdowns. He couldn't actually boast that they merited a 'battle ready' description, but it was clear that a remarkable job had been done — and it had been done mainly by Decker before Kirk had arrived on the scene.

McCoy had been right; Kirk had come to realize that, too. Getting Starship command again had been a secret obsession, hidden even from himself until the Intruder alert occurred. When he realized that this could mean not only returning to space again but also to Enterprise, he had closed his mind to everything else. Retaining command of Enterprise had somehow become for him the purpose of the entire mission. He was genuinely shocked now as he realized how close he had come to defiling an entire lifetime's beliefs.

Kirk had come to the bridge to confront himself on a decision which had now become inescapable – *were Enterprise and Earth best served with himself or Decker in the center seat?* But even as he asked himself that question, he realized that the decision had already been made – he could feel it in the measured, easy way he was breathing, moving, . . . yes, and *thinking*. He knew this feeling – and he was immeasurably gratified that it was still there. It was some stranger who had lived that other life down there. The James Kirk he wanted to be, *the one he was now*, had never left this bridge.

CHAPTER SIXTEEN

Captain's log, stardate 7413.9. Navigational scanners have picked up Intruder and out plot indicates no change in Intruder velocity or heading. We expect a visual within five minutes.

As Kirk completed his log entry, Decker handed him the status readouts. He scanned it, turned toward the helm.

'Navigational scans off; reduce navigational deflections to minimum,' Kirk ordered.

'Forward scans off,' Sulu said. 'Deflectors to minimum.'

Kirk's eyes scanned the bridge, checking off station by station that nothing on the starship could possibly indicate that they were either planning or expecting an attack. It had been as small a thing as a sensor scan which had brought on the destruction of Epsilon Nine. Kirk turned to the helm.

'Navigator?'

'I have a conic interception and pursuit course laid in, sir,' Ilia said.

'Linguacode?'

'We are transmitting basic friendship code and standing by with full-range repeats, sir,' reported Uhura.

Kirk checked to see that Spock was at the science station and relief crew members were at all emergency positions. McCoy came in and fixed himself behind Kirk's shoulder.

'Are we full mag on viewer?' Kirk asked.

'Full mag,' Sulu confirmed. 'Still nothing in sight, sir.'

They would see something soon enough with the huge cloud moving toward them at warp seven and themselves moving toward the cloud even faster. The incredible speed of their combined closure rate was complicated by the unusual mechanics of hyperspace, and an eyeblink of a navigational error could see them flashing past the Intruder-cloud and a million stars past it. But Kirk had confidence in the Deltan.

The *conic interception* to be used would see them passing to one side, but always with the 'nose' of the Enterprise headed at the center of the strange cloud. Thus, as Enterprise passed the cloud, the starship would be traveling sideways but still heading directly toward it until the starship's path took it in directly behind the cloud, almost as if attached to it by a rubber string. Once behind the cloud, Enterprise could overtake it from the rear, permitting Kirk to approach the cloud as slowly or as rapidly as he chose. To anyone looking out the nose of the starship, the conic interception would make it appear that they had always been approaching the cloud head-on but more and more slowly as they got close to it.

The Klingons had not intercepted the cloud this way. Kirk hoped that any star-traveling intelligence would immediately understand the Enterprise maneuver for the peaceful interception that it was.

'Do you see it, sir?' It was Decker asking. Kirk realized that a hush had fallen over the bridge some seconds ago.

'Thank you, Mister Decker. Commander Uhura, you can begin transmitting full range friendship signals.'

Kirk was glad that he had remembered that communications were to be expanded on sighting the cloud. Otherwise, Will Decker might have suspected that the man who replaced him was daydreaming at this significant moment. Yes, he did have it in sight now, too. It was hardly a pinpoint of just slightly warmer a color than the coalesced star mass ahead.

'Go to red alert,' Kirk said quietly. The Klaxon went off. He knew it was no louder than the internal alarms sounding in the minds of the crew. They had all been on the Rec Deck and seen what they would soon be facing – the cloud was beginning to grown in size already – they had also seen the green *death* which emerged from it to destroy a formation of three Klingon starships, each one of them at least nearly as strong as the Enterprise.

'All decks show red alert, sir.' It was Decker reporting vessel status. Kirk gave the nod he knew was expected and turned his mind back to the life or death need of convincing the Intruder that this interception was peaceful. The Enterprise must not appear to be preparing for battle – it was critical that no scan or beam was being emitted by any station on the starship. But it would only show nervousness on his part to ask each ship station if they were certain that this scanner or that sensor was turned off. Besides, it was unnecessary! Decker would have made doubly certain of all that by now, anyway. Kirk came near a smile as he realized how much he was learning to trust the abilities of the young man he had replaced.

The cloud was growing to the size of a fingernail now. Had he forgotten any last minute detail? Kirk let his eyes rest briefly at each bridge station – helm, navigation, science, communications, environment, weapons-defense – he went on to complete the circuit.

The cloud had grown from a pinpoint to the size of a large coin. The crew had also seen death from that cloud destroy Starfleet comrades at Epsilon Nine and it was certain that some of them were beginning to feel some fear. But they were also undoubtedly the most experienced crew ever gathered together – frightened or not, they would obey his commands. And Enterprise was the most sophisticated and powerful starship in the fleet. Kirk felt more certain than ever that he had done the right thing in taking her over. Decker was a fine ship commander, but he did not have Kirk's advantage of having been built by Starfleet into a legendary figure. However irksome and foolish that had been, it meant that Kirk had a crew welded together by the belief (Kirk hoped fervently he would make it true) that they were superbly led.

Kirk felt a rush of sentiment for these men and women here who had seen death strike from that cloud and had still stayed. The 'ordinary' and lovely blue-and-white planet behind them deserved protection – it had bred a sturdy and decent race, certainly a courageous one. From the beginning of time, other groups like this had gone out, handfuls of puny humans standing together against the dark night, against saber-toothed killers, against the sea, and finally into space. The shape and face of the *unknown* had changed during all those eons. but there had been no change in human courage.

'Captain, we are being scanned,' reported Spock.

Kirk touched his ship announcement button. 'All decks, this is the Captain speaking. We are being scanned. Whatever your station, you will do nothing; repeat you will take *no* action except on my express order.'

The cloud was outgrowing the hyperspace star mass ahead, taking its own shape so rapidly that their eyes could see it expanding. Its eerie luminescence was becoming very noticeable.

'The scans are emanating from *exact* cloud center,' reported Spock. 'They consist of an energy effect of an entirely unknown type.'

The size of the cloud now blanketed all the stars from view and had grown to fill half of the blackness ahead of them. Kirk could feel the throb of increasing power as Enterprise continued its conic interception. Although the cloud appeared on the viewer to be straight ahead of them, they were actually passing to one side of it and would soon begin to slide behind it into a pursuit heading.

'The Klingons were first hit at about this distance,' said Decker quietly to Kirk.

What had been *luminscence* before could now be seen to be the result of lovely combinations of multi-hued patterns in the cloud. It was beginning to look its true size now – the cloud's diameter had been reported by young Branch as *an incredible eighty times the Earth-to-sun distance! Big enough to hide a fair-sized star with planets of its own! Its patterned colors were growing in brilliance as the cloud began to dominate all of celestial space ahead of them.*

'Have you sensed any awareness of our presence, Mister Spock?'

Spock shook his head. 'Negative, Captain. Nothing.'

Kirk gave Uhura a questioning look.

'Continuing linguacode peace signals on all frequencies, sir. No reply.'

This was the part of all this which troubled him most. Any intelligence capable of star travel should have no problem translating linguacode. Its keys were universal constants like pi, simple molecular relationships, the speed of light – adolescents with schoolroom computers could easily make sense of it.

Every eye was on the main viewer. If something were going to attack Enterprise, it would happen soon.

'Five minutes to cloud boundary,' Ilia was saying.

'Pursuit acceleration now at warp eight point eight,' reported Sulu.

'Still no reply to friendship messages.' Uhura's voice, like Sulu's, reflected the strain they were all feeling. The naked-headed Deltan female appeared as devoid of emotion now as a Vulcan. Then Kirk became aware that the Vulcan's face *was* showing a flicker of expression. Spock seemed to be astonished by a reading at his console.

'Sir,' Spock said, rechecking the reading, 'I have a preliminary estimate of a twelfth power energy field emanating from the cloud . . .'

'*Twelfth* power?' Sulu interrupted in disbelief.

Kirk was feeling the same surprise. *Twelfth power* energy was on a scale that could stop the Earth's sun from rotating!

'There is definitely an *object* at the heart of the cloud,' Spock continued.

Kirk felt his muscles tightening, reacting to his thought that if the Intruder did not fire soon, then it understood Enterprise's interception course to be peaceful. They were so close to the cloud now that its color patterns had a fierce glow, yet they were still uncountable trillions of trillions of kilometers away.

'Four minutes to cloud boundary,' reported Ilia.

The Enterprise was overtaking the cloud now from directly behind. The ship's engines were beginning to reduce power. Surely any star traveler could not miss seeing that they intended to overtake the cloud very slowly.

The alarm Klaxon sounded.

'Incoming fire. Ahead zero mark zero,' said the computer voice.

They could see it erupting out of the cloud, a tiny point of writhing green energy. It was coming directly toward them.

CHAPTER SEVENTEEN

'Evasive maneuvers!' ordered Kirk.

Sulu's hands were moving controls before the words were completed. Ilia's fingers danced across the navigation computer keys in order to record and project the *hyperspace* complexities of their maneuvers.

'Engine room, stand by for emergency power,' called Decker into the intercom.

On the main viewer, a tiny sparkle of green seemed to float lazily toward them. Kirk knew that the bolt's enormous speed would become apparent only in the last seconds before impact – in the last instant it would seem to rush in and expand into its true size. He heard the computer count *twenty seconds*.

'We have full on forward deflectors, full forcefields, sir,' said Decker from Kirk's side. Kirk could see Chekov's readouts as easily as could Decker, but it was an executive officer's job to ensure that the captain had all vital information regardless of any diversions to his attention.

The main viewer showed the luminescent cloud's patterns tilting and moving across the screen as the evasive maneuvers took Enterprise in a great sweeping curve. Then, at the most advantageous vector-instant, her mighty engines surged into *warp nine emergency power*.

The Intruder's whiplash bolt followed. *It followed easily, effortlessly.*

It hit. *It engulfed!* Its shock wave pierced the starship's protective forcefields, reverberated through the thick titanium hull to where it shook flesh and stunned eardrums with a *deafening energy shriek*. Kirk's adrenaline glands convulsed, shocking his heart into panic beating – for an instant his mind and body were numb with fear.

As Kirk fought to regain control of himself, the deafening shriek continued with an almost demoniacal quality, and he could see it was affecting nearly everyone similarly. Although they had all seen the images of these whiplash bolts destroying Klingon cruisers, nothing could compare with the incredible reality of actually being hit by one. Their starship was shuddering sickeningly; raging green hellfire outside was clinging to the ship's deflector screens and forcefields like a live thing, clawing wildly at the starship's defenses, trying to find some unprotected weakness.

Kirk's mind flashed the thought that if he lived, he must discuss the tactial implications of this shock effect with Heihachiro Nogura. The shocking surprise of being suddenly hit in space with a deafening sound like this was worth considering in future weapons-defense designs.

Kirk twisted around for a quick look at Spock and found him seeming to be at prayer – then the very absurdity of that made him realize the Vulcan was in mind-search of the intelligence which was attacking them. In the other direction, Kirk could see Sulu forcing his eyes and fingers to coordinate as he put Enterprise back on its interception heading with the cloud. Others were forcing their attention back to their jobs, too. Kirk could feel cold perspiration running down his back as he willed himself to sit there giving the appearance of calmness which he knew was needed of him – especially at this moment.

Decker had recovered as quickly as Kirk and had clearly been relieved to see that he was not the only one stunned into an instant of wild fear. He had to tap Kirk's shoulder for his attention; it was impossible to shout above the sound. The exec was indicating the bridge engineering panel which showed the enormous power drain being required to keep their forcefields intact – power reserves were down almost to sixty percent and still dropping.

In the engine room, Montgomery Scott was surprised to see that his grip on the master engine control panel was knuckle-white. It was not being caused by the whiplash energy shriek – the emergency acceleration to warp nine during evasive maneuvers had been almost equally deafening down here. It was the reserve power readings that troubled Scott – they were not *below fifty percent*. He had no choice but to shut off the deflectors and divert all power to the vessel's main forcefield screens.

Damn! At the very instant he switched over, the image of a green flicker had seemed to flash into view past one of Scott's hull monitors. Then he saw the flashing alarm lights which showed a rapid chain of short-outs, as if something were forcing its way through the vessel's main circuitry!

Assistant Engineer Kugel attracted Scott's attention, indicating on the main board where the effect appeared to be weakening as bits of it split off to follow the vessel's circuitry in different directions.

Then a piece of it found a route to the engine room – writhing green fire spat out of an auxiliary console. Kugel almost got out of its way in time, but a wispy green bit of it touched him – and he screamed.

On the bridge, the security console operator was

puzzling over INTRUDER ALERT readings which were appearing along the path of the vessel's mainbus circuitry. Then she realized what it must be and where part of it was heading – but she had no time to give a warning.

A dying green flicker spurted from the weapons-defense console – it was enough to cling briefly to Chekov's right arm, sending him writhing to the deck. The automatic fire-damping controls engaged immediately, and through the spraying fog, Chekov's agony could be heard.

Decker went between Kirk and Sulu, vaulting the railing to take over Chekov's vital weapons-defense duties. Kirk saw Ilia hurrying to Chekov's immediate aid, which was correct emergency procedure since her navigator's console would continue providing and recording data without her presence.

It was fading away! Then the whiplash bolt was gone, and its ear-splitting sound with it!

'The new forcefields held!' Sulu breathed the words in relief. In the background, the turbolift doors snapped open long enough for Doctor Chapel to hurry in, reaching into her emergency medical kit as she raced toward the injured Chekov.

'Engineering to bridge,' called the chief engineer. 'We are down to only a fraction over thirty percent reserve power!'

Kirk had really not hoped for more – Scott went on to give the captain a quick, common sense analysis of their situation. Kirk accepted the recommendations, which included diverting all but the barest necessary power from gravity control, the inertial dampeners, and life support. Even then, Kirk doubted they could withstand more than five or six seconds of another whiplash attack.

'It held onto us a full twenty-six seconds following

impact,' reported Decker, as if reading Kirk's mind. Both men knew that they had another six seconds of forcefield power at most – another attack would finish them.

On the deck at weapons defense, Chapel had spray-hypoed Chekov with as much pain relief as was safe. She was about to turn and summon help when the Deltan navigator touched her arm. 'I was working to stop his pain when you arrived,' Ilia said. 'Let me finish.'

There was something in the Deltan female's look that made Chapel nod and move aside. Ilia took Chekov's head in her hands, putting her fingers to his temples. Then Chapel saw a faintly surprised look form on Chekov's face and his body began to relax. Chapel knew of the physiological similarities between ecstasy and pain, of course, and she knew generally that there was some psionic sharing of consciousness between Deltans during sexual experience, but it came as a surprise to see that Ilia had been able to extend her own consciousness into Chekov's mind and help depress his perception of pain.

Spock's eyes came open and he turned heavily toward Kirk. He could not remember ever having felt so exhausted. 'Captain, I have sensed . . . puzzlement. We *have* been contacted. Why have we not replied?'

Uhura was whirling in that direction, shocked. 'That's impossible, Mister Spock. I'm using constant *scan and search* on all possible frequencies.'

'The Intruder *has* been attempting to communicate,' insisted Spock. 'Whatever the method was, it is imperative we locate the message.' Spock was at his console again, his hands moving rapidly over his complex keyboards as he programmed computer searches through transceiver recordings. Uhura had raced back to her console and was making her own rapid search.

Kirk threw a fast look at the cloud patterns on the main viewscreen – they were almost there already. *If* they could find the message, it would have to be translated, they would have to reply, the Intruder would have to translate their reply. . . . How long would they be given before another whiplash bolt came at them?

The image of the luminescent cloud had long ago spilled past the confines of the bridge's main viewer. All Sulu could do was keep it aimed at the exact cloud center to give them every possible instant of warning when another attack emerged.

Kirk realized that his only other choice was to turn away and appear to abandon direct interception. But with the cloud now less than twenty-four hours from Earth, the loss of even more hours as he maneuvered would be . . .

The Klaxon sounded.

'Incoming fire, heading zeo mark zero,' said the computer voice.

Kirk saw the dot of green as it emerged from the cloud. 'Spock,' he said, 'can anyone help you?'

'Negative,' said Spock.

'Impact in twenty seconds,' said the Deltan navigator.

Kirk had always wondered what he would think about on the day he saw death inevitable. He found that the answer to that was almost ridiculously simple – he was annoyed, especially as he realized he might have lived another full century, assuming no accidents or . . .

He became aware of a repeated, shrill, incredibly fast beep. He whirled, turning to be greeted by a confirming nod from Spock. It was coming from the direction of the science console!

'Patching into your console now, Mister Spock,' Uhura was saying.

'Fifteen seconds to impact,' reported Ilia.

'Frequency more than one million megahertz,' Spock was saying rapidly. 'At such speed, their entire message lasted only a millisecond.'

'No time now to translate their message,' said Decker.

'We will repeat our standard linguacode signal,' said Spock. 'Now programming to send it at their transmission speed.'

Kirk sat waiting, helpless. Spock would work as rapidly as possible without urging.

'Ten seconds,' said Ilia.

Finally, Spock hit a button and a millisecond beep sounded.

'Transmitting,' reported Decker to Kirk.

'*Five* seconds,' Ilia stated clearly.

The writhing energy bolt was upon them, flaring large . . . but did not strike. At the last instant, just as its whiplash fury was filling the viewscreen, *it simply faded from sight*.

The relief was almost as shocking as the first bolt's deafening shrillness. There were no cheers, and at first the looks between one and the other were still so numbed as to be almost uncomprehending.

'It appears that our friendship messages have been received and understood,' said Spock blandly.

'Thank you, Mister Spock.'

'One minute to cloud boundary,' reported the Deltan navigator.

'Maintain present heading,' ordered Kirk.

CHAPTER EIGHTEEN

The wispy edges of the cloud had looked like gigantic *aurora borealis* effects, the Enterprise whipping past and through transparent and towering graceful draperies of transparent colored light.

'Full power on navigational scanners and deflectors,' ordered Kirk to Ilia.

'Full on scanners and deflectors, sir.'

Until now, they had been using navigational deflectors at minimum power, accepting the risk of encountering large asteroids or other heavy space debris. Kirk had feared that the Intruder could mistake full power navigational deflectors for the forcefield defenses of a battle-ready vessel. And, of course, the navigational scanners searching far in advance of their path for space hazards might be mistaken for a sensor scan – it had been a sensor scan by Epsilon Nine which had triggered the destruction of that outpost station.

Tension. Except for Spock, every eye on the bridge was on the viewer in the hope that green death would not appear out of all this loveliness. But the risk had to be taken – the cloud was large enough to hide literally anything, even a star with planets, and they needed scanners to detect and alter the vessel's course to avoid hazards too large to be handled by the deflectors. The scanners were also vital in locating whatever was at the heart of the cloud, and in guiding them into a parallel course with it. They had sent high-speed linguacode transmissions explaining all this, but had received no reply.

The actual entry into the cloud was even more spectacular than the approach. At the last instant, it appeared so filled with brilliant patterned color that they seemed to be plunging headlong into a giant star. There had been the sensation of a slight impact – Kirk thought it felt strangely like a clean entry into the water after a good dive. The Enterprise seemed to be riding into it on the crest of a great wave of colors, a breaking wave that crashed, tumbling the colors into streamers and globules which slowly faded and disappeared into the unrelieved white brilliance of the cloud's interior. The Enterprise became like a white paper submersible exploring a sea of milk.

The phenomenal color displays of cloud entry had been like a pyrotechnics celebration of their success in arriving there. Despite whatever might await them at the center of the cloud some twenty minutes ahead, the bridge crew felt themselves relaxing a bit – for the time they had done all they could do until they met whatever lay hidden ahead.

Decker indicated the main viewer to Spock. 'Are you still convinced that the cloud is a powerfield?'

'There is no longer any doubt of that,' Spock announced from his science console.

'Even assuming the possibility of a powerfield this large,' challenged Decker, 'it still doesn't explain what makes it *visible*.'

'The annihilation of hydrogen atoms,' said Spock. 'At the Intruder's velocity, there are more than enough free atoms in space to create a visible effect.'

Decker pointed out that it would take nearly unimaginable power from something at the heart of the cloud to annihilate free hydrogen on a scale like this – and he challenged Spock for an explanation of how a mere powerfield could destroy hydrogen atoms in such a way as to produce the mixed colors and patterns they had seen. The Vulcan replied that the power source was no doubt as complex as it was powerful.

'Are you suggesting it could be a fleet of vessels, Mister Spock?' This from Chekov at weapons defense.

'Perhaps even an armada,' Spock answered.

Then the Vulcan had seemed to realize he was near to feeling a human enjoyment of the discussion and he had gone immedately back into his self-imposed shell. He had stayed there through the long minutes that followed as the Enterprise continued decelerating, slowly probing its way toward cloud center.

'I read a large object . . .' Ilia stopped, uncertain of what her navigational scanners were actually showing. 'Unable to say for certain what this reading means.'

'A fast sensor scan?' Decker had suggested.

Kirk shook his head. There had been no choice but to use navigational aids. But a sensor scan might still be considered an invasion of privacy. No, sensor scans were not vital – at least not yet.

Kirk was surprised to see the cloud apparently thinning toward its center. They passed through a small, clear area, then a larger one.

'Like the calm weather at the eye of a hurricane,' said Uhura.

Then they saw something! Sulu's hands went to the emergency maneuvering controls with a blur of speed, but a long filament of cloud immediately hid the object from view again. Sulu hesitated, his hands ready – his reaction had been like that of a winged craft pilot sighting an unexpected mountain peak in the clouds.

They saw another gigantic shape. 'That's two of them . . .' began Sulu.

'It is all part of the same object,' interrupted Ilia. The Deltan navigator indicated the proof of this on her scanner reading.

'Hold this relative position,' said Kirk quickly. He had seen them approaching another larger 'hole' in the cloud, and his order was timed to bring the Enterprise into the clearing as its relative motion stopped. Their course and velocity were now exactly the same as the unbelievable bulk which looked out ahead of them, continuing to where it was obscured by fragments of cloud in the distance.

'Distance to object is seventy thousand kilometers,' reported Ilia.

Whatever it was, it was huge enough to be almost beyond comprehension.

They were on the same scale to it that a mosquito would be approach their own starship. What could be seen of the object appeared generally to be an oblate spheroid shape – its surface had a strange shimmering texture as if it held uncountable details which at this distance could not be made out separately.

For all his experience with alien vessels, some of them enormous, Kirk's mind at first refused to accept that this could be called a vessel. It was the largest thing he had ever encountered in space, bigger than the largest orbital cities. He had readied himself to face the spectacular, even the terrifying – but this was the unimaginable. If this is a ship, thought Kirk, it is the apotheosis of all ships. If a god should ever build a ship, it would be like this one.

Uhura whirled toward him. 'Captain, negative contact with Starfleet. Transmissions will no longer penetrate either in or out of the cloud.'

'Activate a message drone,' Kirk ordered. 'Send these images and our current status.'

'I make its dimensions as . . . seventy-eight kilometres in length,' Decker was saying.

Almost *eighty kilometers* – the vessel out there was double the length of old Manhattan Island!

'It could have a crew of thousands, *hundreds* of thousands,' said Ilia.

'Or just a few of them hundreds of meters tall,' said Sulu.

'No reply to our hailing signals,' reported Uhura. She had been transmitting them at the Intruder's high speed rate, through a full spectrum of frequencies.

'Message drones launched,' Chekov said.

Kirk turned to Ilia and Sulu. 'Give us a three minute closure to within a hundred kilometers of Intruder.'

Ilia put it on the course plot instantly. The others looked toward Kirk nervously, even Spock giving him a glance, a raised eyebrow, as Sulu touched his maneuvering controls.

'Beginning approach to Intruder,' said Sulu.

The starship's parallel course changed only slightly, but the new heading had it angling closer toward the immense alien.

As they moved closer and the alien vessel continued to grow in size, the texture of its surface began to resolve itself into highly detailed fine patterns. At the science console, Spock had seen enough and he was now sitting in meditation, apparently in hopes of again contacting the consciousness which had seemed to him to fit the proportions of that alien vessel. Decker was crossing back from Chekov's console where he had been using the ranging optics.

'Estimate it as two hundred fifty-seven times our length, sir,' said Decker, quietly. 'It's displacement calculates as about *six million* times larger than us.'

Still closer, the alien vessel was growing impossibly huge; its outer 'texture' had become complex patterns of . . . of *what*? The complexity of its surface was as incredible as it gigantic size. Kirk wondered if some of what he was seeing could be solid sheets of subatomic particles. At another place the surface seemed to be walls of energy – yet how could energy act like matter?

Decker's thoughts were racing along similar lines. Was he seeing *coherent matter*? It was barely a possibility in some scientists' minds. It might be possible for a very highly advanced technology to organize matter in parallel, disciplined sheets to become thousands or perhaps millions of times stronger than any ordinary substance. Decker was grateful to have been able to see this, even if it had to be as Enterprise's executive officer rather than her captain. Whatever the outcome, it was a stupendous experience.

'What is our distance?' asked Kirk.

'Nine hundred sixty kilometers and still closing,' replied Sulu.

It seemed impossible to Kirk that they could still be so far away. The alien vessel loomed like a small moon. But its crew had given no indication yet of any unhappiness at their close approach. Kirk was aware, uncomfortably aware, that the Intruder's warp velocity would have it and them entering Earth's solar system in less than a day now. He did not have time for a leisurely investigation.

He had to make contact with the life forms there – *force* contact if necessary.

'Mister Spock,' said Kirk, 'we're going to risk sensors. Begin with a low-grade surface scan.'

'Aye, Captain,' replied Spock.

Kirk heard the low hum of the scanners as they came on – then everything on the bridge was blasted by a blinding explosion of light.

Blinding – literally, and still continuing. Kirk shielded his eyes with his hands, then fought to see through his slitted fingers. He could hear a loud, undulating humming sound – bright patterns danced and flickered as he slowly regained vision and began to make out a presence – *an alien presence which was standing on his bridge!*

'I believe it to be composed of plasma-energy,' said Spock over the sound of the thing.

As Kirk's eyes adjusted to the glare of it, he could see that it was not actually *standing* on the bridge – it floated there. And plasma-energy seemed as good a description as any. It was a swirling mass of dull red and violet mixed with brilliant flashes which stabbed at the bridge crew's eyes like white-hot needles. It was double the thickness of a big man and about a head taller.

'I believe it to be a form of machine,' added Spock. 'Perhaps a probe sent to investigate us.'

Spock was right. Or so it appeared to Kirk, whose eyes were adjusting well enough to make out shadowy whirling and pumping movements within the red-purple swirl of plasma. It had the look of intricate mechanisms created out of different kinds or grades of energy.

No panic on the bridge. Kirk was grateful he had experienced people here. But the plasma-energy thing seemed totally oblivious to the bridge crew. As it floated toward the center of the bridge, a technician edged out of its way and was ignored. Then it stopped moving – a 'tendril' of plasma lashed out, almost a cobra-strike movement, narrowly missing Uhura's head as it *fastened itself into her communications console*. All the console read-outs flashed on brightly – the frightening energy thing was obviously activating the entire console, exploring all its functions.

'Stand clear of all bridge positions!'

Kirk gave the order just in time as still another tendril lashed out and fastened into the bridge engineering console, which lit up brightly, too – then another snaked out and entered the starship's helm controls as Sulu rolled clear just in time.

The probe hovered near the bridge center, its ominous hum louder as its tendrils entered console after console. It looked like some great energy-octopus, starved and feeding ravenously off the information being sucked from the starship control circuitry.

Kirk was on his feet and Spock came to his side as the elevator doors snapped open and a pair of security guards burst in.

'No weapons!' Chekov shouted the warning immediately, but it came too late – one of the guards had raised his phaser and a tiny version of the green whiplash bolt roiled across the bridge. The security man *vanished*. The second guard carefully returned his phaser to his belt as Chekov gave a fast intercom warning that no more security personnel were to be sent.

Some consoles were going dark again as the plasma-energy probe withdrew its tendrils – it was floating over to hover near Chekov.

'Don't interfere with it!' Decker warned.

'*Absolutely* I will not interfere!' promised Chekov fervently. The probe inserted one of its energy tendrils into Chekov's console, directly past his face.

'It is not interested in *us*,' Kirk murmured, 'only in the ship.'

'Fascinating,' said Spock. 'What better way to examine a vessel than from its control-center here?'

The probe seemed to become aware of some information it had not investigated yet. All other tendrils had withdrawn and the thing now floated in Kirk's and Spock's direction.

'Watch out!'

A much heavier tendril snaked out to the science console complex, which flashed brightly into life and began to yield information. The Kirk reacted, alarmed, as he saw the science computer flash into life, too – Spock's computer was the only one which interconnected directly with the starship's main computer.

'Computer off!' Kirk snapped. The science computer ignored the voice command.

Decker edged past the tendril hitting the computer's manual shut-down switch, but without result. 'It won't switch off, Captain. It's taken control of it!'

'It's running our records. Starfleet strength, Earth defenses . . .' Kirk trailed his words helplessly.

Spock was in motion. Even as Kirk spoke, the Vulcan was locking his hands together overhead and now he brought them down in a tremendous two-handed chop into the computer pedestal.

The entire face of the console *shattered* . . . bridge lights dimmed as the panel was shorted out.

Spock pivoted, attempting to back away fast, but an energy tendril brushed him – a pinpoint green flash at the contact point sent the Vulcan spinning under the rail and down at Ilia's feet. A thick energy tendril followed after him.

'Mister Spock, don't move!'

The Deltan navigator Ilia was stepping past Spock, trying to distract the probe's attention. She succeeded.

'*Ilia!*' It was Decker shouting a warning, *but the probe enveloped Ilia, exploding into blinding white light again, and disappeared, taking Ilia with it*. A tricorder fell to the deck – it was the one she had been holding in her hand.

CHAPTER NINETEEN

Ilia's tricorder hit the deck and rolled over twice before lying still. In that same time, Decker's eyes had taken in the fact she was indisputably gone and he was turning toward Uhura.

'Linguacode, high speed! Tell them that it is a life form they've just taken from our ship; transmit Deltan life support requirements!'

Kirk caught Decker's eye and nodded agreement with the urgency of the message. Undoubtedly, they should have sent a similar message when the security man Phillips disappeared. They had simply assumed that the bright flash of his disappearance was destruction. But since both the plasma-energy probe and Ilia had vanished together, it was more likely that the brilliant flash was part of some transportation process doing much the same job as the Enterprise's transporter chambers. Meanwhile, the agony in Decker's expression made it clear that he was feeling greater affection for Ilia than he had realized he carried.

The main viewer showed that Sulu had the Enterprise still on a parallel course with the immense alien, keeping position at a full one hundred kilometers away – and even at this distance, the enormous bulk of the other vessel more than filled the big viewer screen. Kirk could hear Uhura sending repeats of the life support information on Ilia. Spock turned back to his science console and began to run the low-power sensor scans which Kirk had ordered only seconds before the frightening plasma-energy appeared.

Kirk struggled to think clearly and consecutively about all this. Had they angered the aliens when Spock shorted out the probe's examination of Enterprise's computer-library? Possibly, but Kirk doubted that the plasma-energy probe left for that reason, or that it snatched up Ilia out of pique. It was maddening to be uncertain of everything when the Intruders were clearly able to communicate with the Enterprise had they wished to do so.

The Enterprise suddenly wrenched sideways. Even Spock showed some signs of being startled. It was as if something had yanked at them.

'Tractor beam?' Decker was making a quick guess.

'Tractor beam confirmed,' said Spock. One of his monitors was showing the play of force which was exerting pressure on the ship's hull.

'Red alert?' asked Decker.

Kirk shook his head; the Enterprise was still on yellow alert, all critical emergency stations were manned. Battle with the alien vessel was unthinkable – except as a last desperate resort.

On the main viewer the image of the alien continued growing – as the tractor beam pulled them still closer. Decker was calling for a relief crewman to take over at the navigator's console.

'Engineering, full emergency power!' Kirk snapped the order into the intercom and got an immediate confirmation from Montgomery Scott.

They could feel the Enterprise straining as she tried to break free of whatever force held her in its grip.

'Engineer to bridge, I can't hold this power long. Intermix chamber is heating up fast . . .'

Spock studied his readings, then turned to pronounce a verdict. 'We cannot break free, Captain. We do not have a fraction of the power necessary.'

'Belay emergency power, Scotty.'

'Aye, sir. What in the hell has got hold of us?'

Kirk ignored Scott's question. Whatever it was, it make him uneasy to be so totally helpless. He had a vision of some gigantic alien child-thing over there reeling in a tiny minnow it had caught, and which it might soon flay open and examine.

'Spock! Are you sensing anything?!' Then Kirk saw the Vulcan's eyebrow go up a trifle. He realized that he had almost shouted the question and immediately regretted it. Whatever happened, he must be able to view it coolly and dispassionately. *The Intruder vessel was pulling them very close! Why?*

The replacement navigator entered the bridge on a run, Decker monitoring her to the empty station. She gave one look to the frightening image on the bridge viewer, then began quickly orientating herself to Ilia's board.

McCoy arrived on the bridge, tried to avoid looking startled as he took in the viewer image. 'Well,' he said grimly to Kirk, 'it looks like they've decided to examine us.' Kirk felt a gut chill as he remembered his invented image of a gigantic child-alien slicing the Enterprise open.

It was costing Decker some effort to appear to be making a routine executive officer's bridge circuit, and Kirk admired the success with which he was pulling it off. Chekov was glancing at Decker as if wondering if he'd gone mad.

Kirk looked quickly back to the viewer. *It was drawing them in rapidly; they were coming critically close to it. Had they annoyed it into angrily crushing them against its side?*

It was almost instinct to turn quickly to Spock for his assessment – but what was wrong with Spock? His head was turned to one side, his eyes fixed on . . . on what? Then Kirk realized that Spock was again attempting mind-contact. Kirk hoped desperately that it was with the Intruder aliens.

'I read deceleration!' said Sulu, relieved. 'They're pulling us in more slowly.'

They had been brought in to less than a hundred meters away, and were being pulled along the incredible length of the alien colossus. There was not even a whispered word from a bridge crew member as they watched and almost disbelieved what their eyes showed them. It would have been difficult to describe what they were seeing as the 'hull' of a ship. Some of it could hardly be called even a 'surface', being more like great swirling 'ponds' of an unknown and impossible *energy substance*.

My God, it was opening up! Up ahead, there was a seam of light near the aft end of the huge vessel, which was widening into an almost mouth-like shape.

'Oh, *no* . . .!' Someone's voice had quivered it.

'It's opening like a *maw*!' This from Sulu, being forced out of him in shocked surprise.

Kirk could feel ripples of terror begin to circle the bridge. Sulu had made an unfortunate choice of the word 'maw', although the helmsman could hardly be blamed for describing the look of it so accurately. Any moment, panic might sweep the entire starship – Kirk knew that one of the primal human fears was that of being devoured by some other gigantic creature.

McCoy headed for the elevators, calling over his shoulder to Chekov: 'Get medical observers to all decks! Fast!'

'All decks, attention,' Kirk keyed his intercom, trying to sound matter-of-fact. 'This is the Captain speaking. It should be obvious that the vessel out there could have destroyed us long ago if its crew meant us any harm. It seems probable that we are being moved to a place, a compartment of their vessel, possibly – where we hope communication between us and them can be facilitated.' Kirk knew that his announcement, laced with *probably* and *possibly*, really said nothing, but he could already see some relief on a couple of faces; apparently it had helped to remind everyone that this was merely an enormous vessel out there. He managed to smile at his own gallows humor – *merely* a vessel?

On the main viewer, the opening had widened large enough to accommodate several Enterprises. And they were close enough to see that the 'gaping mouth' was actually the beginning of a vast chamber which extended a dozen or so kilometers ahead into the incredible alien vessel. Apparently a 'compartment' of the vast ship was dimly and intermittently lit by eerie 'powerfield eruptions' which appeared and vanished in there like heat lightning.

'We're being pulled through with ample clearance on all sides.' It was the replacement navigator checking her maneuver-monitor. Kirk gave her an approving glance, searching for the name – yes, *DiFalco*. There might be something about her worth remembering.

'Your estimate of this, Exec?' asked Kirk. 'They seem to be taking care not to damage us.'

'Agreed, Captain,' said Decker. 'I'd guess that they want a closer look at us. It should be interesting to see what they look like.'

Then they were inside.

Kirk looked up to see that Spock was standing beside him. There was fatigue visible on the Vulcan features as he examined the main viewer image.

Uhura, shuddering, pointed at the gargantuan sheets of ragged-edged forcefields which they were being pulled past. 'They look like *teeth*. . . .'

'They are *not* teeth,' snapped Kirk. Nevertheless, he found himself glancing at Spock for confirmation.

Spock was still peering at the main viewer. Then he announced: 'I sensed *insatiable curiosity*, Captain.'

Kirk frowned at the viewer image – was something changing? 'Reverse direction on viewer,' he called.

'Reverse on viewer,' replied Sulu as he punched in a rear view. *The 'maw' was closing behind them. Trapped?* The word was on everyone's face.

'Viewer ahead,' said Kirk quietly.

'I believe they have a bottomless hunger for knowledge,' Spock was continuing. It was a hunger which Spock shared; he wondered if this was a thread which could lead to some kinship.

'Recommend we stand by on maneuvering thrusters, just in case.' This from Decker, and Kirk nodded his agreement to Sulu.

'Also, give us a scan, helmsman. Let's have a look around in here.'

The main viewer began to show that this was, as Kirk had believed, a vast 'compartment' within the great vessel – enough room for a fair-sized city. And yet, its vastness was not really *empty*, not during every moment, at least. Unusual shapes and patterns appeared and vanished continually, undoubtedly representing some incredible technology which apparently used *energy* or some form of *energy plasma* much like humans and others used *matter* for constructing bulkheads and engines and other shipboard necessities. This absence of matter, at least as humans understood the word, leant a curious unreality to everything. Sometimes it could be a breathtakingly lovely, colorful ribbon pattern of light – suddenly becoming an enormous explosion of energy, then vanishing as new shapes reappeared here, there, becoming still different shapes. There was a sense of 'order' in it, too – a feeling that all this was merely the smoothly functioning apparatus of this great vessel.

During this, Spock turned to Kirk. 'Permission to use sensors?'

'Affirmative. Begin sensor scans.'

Spock hurried to his science console. It seemed probable to both of them that the aliens would certainly understand their being curious about where they were being taken.

'Their tractor beam has released us, sir,' called Chekov.

'They've brought us to a halt, no forward motion,' said Sulu. 'Standing by on maneuvering thrusters.'

Sulu had brought the main viewer to *ahead*, and it showed a lace-bulwark of powerful patterns closing off any further travel into the alien ship.

'Hold station,' said Kirk to helm.

'Thrusters at station keeping.'

Spock was working rapidly at his console, shifting from one set of readouts to another in a pattern too rapid for

Kirk to follow. Then Spock hit a master control, part of his console going dark. There was a trace of almost human disappointment on his features. 'Captain,' he said, '*all* our scans are being reflected back. Our sensors are useless.'

Kirk acknowledged. 'Have you been able to analyze any part of this?'

'I believe the visible shapes and patterns to be energy fields – undoubtedly part of the vessel's mechanisms.' Was there a touch of awe in Spock's voice? 'A technology so incredibly sophisticated that I cannot . . .'

He was cut off by the voice of the bridge computer: '*Intruder alert . . . Intruder alert . . .!*' There was a stir on the bridge – the recent visit from the aliens' frightening plasma-energy probe was still very much on everyone's mind.

Chekov was reacting to a reading: 'Deck four, Captain; officers' quarters.'

'Spock, anything?'

Spock was shaking his head. 'I have no unusual powerfield readings from there, Captain. I should guess it is *not* their plasma-energy probe this time.'

'I'm getting a *heat reading*, something in the one thousand degrees range . . . no, correct that, nine hundred fifty . . . and still dropping. Whatever's happened down there, it's cooling fairly rapidly.'

Kirk was there, examining Chekov's security console readings. They exchanged a look and Kirk whirled to Decker. 'You have the conn, Will. Come with me, please, Mister Spock!'

CHAPTER TWENTY

A pair of security guards were waiting at the cabin marked 'Ilia, Lt. (NAV) 07719.' Spock's eyebrow came up on seeing the name on the door Kirk had learned from Chekov's panel that the Intruder alert was in their former navigator's quarters, and this had prompted him to leave Decker behind at the conn.

One of the security men had an identity sensor trained on the door. Its tiny monitor was displaying digital readings: 165 . . . 160 . . 155 . . .

'Whatever's in there was white-hot only a few minutes ago,' said a security officer.

'Fascinating,' said Spock. Kirk nodded, aware that the Vulcan referred to the fact that neither smoke or flame alarms had been triggered in there. And since a flare of temperatures that high *should* have caused something to burn, the aliens who had taken Lieutenant Ilia from them must have sent over something unusual to her cabin. Whatever it might be, it was no place for Will Decker, who had reacted with such anguish at the Deltan navigator's disappearance.

Other security details were hurrying in to close off bulkheads and handle the other 'Intruder alert' routines. Kirk motioned to one guard to accompany himself and Spock.

'No weapons,' he cautioned.

Kirk cracked the door open slowly until they could peer into what seemed to be an empty cabin. As he expected, there was no sign of the frightening plasma-energy probe. The aliens certainly realized by now that it was the wrong kind of device for an investigation of the Enterprise crew.

Spock was indicating the guard's identity-sensor read-outs. Whatever was in the cabin, its temperature had dropped to thirty-eight degrees and was beginning to hold steady near that temperature.

As the moved carefully in through the door, Kirk could make out a faint scent of Ilia still lingering in the fabric of her lounge-bed.

'The head source is in the sonic shower,' said Spock.

'What the hell?' Kirk spun quickly toward the cabin's dressing alcove. Through the transparent door of the hydrosonic shower he saw something moving. It was definitely a body – looking very human, or Deltan. *The heat they had read in the cabin there? Had it been some malfunction in the sonic cubicle? Or had something been cooling itself down to normal Enterprise temperatures there?*

Then, whatever it was, it moved closer to the transparent door. It was unmistakably a naked female!

Kirk stepped to the cabin's master control panel, touched the sonics door switch – the transparency slid open. It was *Ilia*! Lovely, almost unbearably lovely in her nudity! Then Kirk felt a warning touch from Spock.

'This is not our navigator,' Spock said quietly.

But it almost certainly *was* Ilia – except that there was some sort of a glowing light from the throat. . . . Kirk found his eyes shifting from the tiny light glow to what seemed impossibly lovely, hard-tipped breasts which were at this moment swinging around to point directly at him . . . *damn! It had to be Deltan pheromones that were doing this to him! This meant Spock was wrong. She had to be Ilia!*

'Ensign,' said Kirk, 'get Doctor McCoy up here fast.'

It took the young security officer a moment to force his eyes away from the Deltan nakedness. Kirk knew how difficult it was. He had just realized that the pointing of those two breasts toward himself had simply meant that she was turning to look toward them. The *eyes*! They seemed devoid of living warmth! Was this somehow *Ilia's dead body*? A corpse, reanimated and controlled by the aliens?

Kirk's direction of thought was bringing his attention back to her naked body – as he stepped toward her in the sonics cubicle. Her cold eyes followed his movements as he punched in a dress code, then slid the transparent door closed long enough for a leisure robe to form over her nakedness.

What was the look Spock had given him? *Amusement* or *pity*? Apparently, Deltan pheromones created no sensual excitement in the Vulcan; otherwise he would have understood the wisdom of putting some garment on her. The transparent door slid open again and the Deltan form spoke.

'*Yurathirkunit?*'

Kirk saw Spock cock an ear as if half understanding. The voice came out ... *unpracticed*? Like something mechanical trying to sound alive?

'You ... are ... the ... Kirk ... unit?'

'Remarkable,' said Spock. 'It learns very fast.'

'I am Captain James T. Kirk, commanding U.S.S. Enterprise,' Kirk replied, feeling somewhat foolish saying this to what looked like his own navigator. *Was Ilia really this incredibly sensuous?*

'I have been programmed to observe and record normal functions of the carbon-based units infesting U.S.S. Enterprise.'

'Programmed by whom?' asked Kirk. 'It is important we communicate with them.'

The probe seemed puzzled. 'If you require a designation, I was programmed by *Vejur*.' Its voice was becoming more understandable, taking on some of their navigator's throaty Deltan vocal tone. The Vulcan was watching it in absolute fascination. But it was intellectual fascination – the Deltan scents were clearly wasted on Vulcans.

'Who is Vejur?' Kirk asked.

'Vejur is that which programmed me.'

'Are you referring to someone in that larger vessel out there? The captain? Or the leader of whoever is aboard it?'

The door opened and McCoy rushed in. 'Jim, what's–?' McCoy's trained eye took her in for only a moment before his medical tricorder came out fast and he began a scan of the female form.

'Who is Vejur?' Kirk repeated.

'Vejur is that which seeks the Creator.'

Kirk had difficulty believing that his ears had heard correctly. The *Creator*? The considerable astonishment on Spock's features said he must have heard these same words, too.

'Jim – this is a mechanism.' It was McCoy, indicating 'Ilia.'

Kirk stared at the ship's doctor. This Deltan female form, as far as his eyes could tell, looked *exactly* real. It had reacted with Deltan sensuality and sexuality by releasing pheromones – and Kirk knew that both he and the security ensign could testify to *their* reality.

Spock was making his own scan with the doctor's tricorder. 'I believe this form replaces the plasma-energy probe which had been sent to examine our vessel, Captain. It may even be the same probe, using the Ilia-pattern it carried back with it . . .'

Kirk turned to the female form, making his question a demand: '*Where is Lieutenant Ilia?*'

'That unit no longer functions.' The mechanism's tone sounded factual. 'I have been given its form to more readily communicate with the carbon-based units infest-ing Enterprise.'

'Carbon-based units?' the security guard said, feeling some ominous undertone.

'Humans, Ensign Chavez,' McCoy said dryly. '*Us.*'

One of Spock's eyebrows had raised at the probe's use of the word 'infesting'. He seemed to find it interesting, but Kirk had a more pressing question which must come first.

'Vejur's ship,' Kirk asked, 'why does it travel in toward the third planet of the solar system directly ahead?'

'Vejur travels to the third planet to find the Creator.'

It stunned them. Whatever *Vejur* might be, some single great *entity* or an entire alien race, it was simply impossible that anything capable of that vessel's technology could believe that Earth was the location of anything that could be called *Creator*.

Kirk tried to pursue it sensibly. 'What is the Creator?' he asked.

'That which creates,' answered the Ilia-probe. The mechanical sound in its voice was almost gone – it also seemed to move more gracefully, as if becoming accus-tomed to the use of the various mechanisms making up its 'body'.

'What does Vejur want of the Creator?'

'To join with Him.'

'Join with the Creator?' Spock asked. 'How?'

'Vejur and the Creator will become One.'

'What does the Creator create?' asked Spock.

'The Creator is that which created Vejur,' the Ilia-probe was saying.

This perfectly circular logic suggested that there might be some considerable communications gulf between them and Vejur – it might be difficult, perhaps impossible, to share common concepts or values. This probe had been sent to study them and it seemed likely to Kirk that any findings accumulated here might be totally uncomprehensible to whatever sent the probe.

'*Who is Vejur?*' Kirk asked again.

'Vejur is that which seeks the Creator.'

Kirk wondered if this might not be the literal truth. The life forms over there were likely to be as advanced as their enormous vessel. Or their probes. What better use of their knowledge and technology than to seek the source of themselves and the universe? Kirk could accept that as philosophically noble and even proper – but he also knew that nothing definable as 'Creator' would be found on that very ordinary planet ahead. And what might happen to that very ordinary world if the crew of that gigantic vessel felt disappointed with it?

The Ilia-probe had apparently waited long enough. 'I am ready to commence my observations,' it said.

'Doctor,' said Spock quickly, 'a thorough examination of this probe might provide insight into those who manufactured it and how to communicate with them.'

McCoy agreed, nodding as he took an 'Ilia' arm to escort it out. He was spun around off balance – the gentle tug on its arm had been like trying to pull a building after him. It ignored McCoy, addressed Kirk. 'I am programmed to observe and record normal functioning procedures of the carbon-based units.'

'The examination *is* a normal function,' Kirk said with his old resourcefulness.

The Ilia-probe considered it a moment. 'You may proceed,' it said.

The examining room medical viewer was showing the probe's 'Ilia' body in near-transparent detail while console monitors revealed closer details. McCoy was muttering in amazement as he ran the scanner over the probe's form. '. . . micro-miniature hydraulics, sensors, molecule-sized multi-processor chips . . . and look at *this*. . . .'

Chapel was equally amazed. 'An osmotic micro-pump here, and here,' she pointed out. 'The smallest body functions are *exactly* duplicated, including the Deltan exocrine system.' She traced with her finger on the screen, indicating the extent of these mechanical replications of Ilia's body.'

Kirk's thoughts had already moved on. He was no longer questioning *how* Vejur had built this probe, but *why*. Why did it need such minute perfection? What use would a probe have for, say, the sexually stimulating *pheromones*, secreting subliminal scents. . . . *He interrupted his thoughts, cursing inwardly, as he felt a warm wave of sexual desire. Damn! Then he realized that the machine was doing something very Deltan and female at this moment. Decker had just entered the examining room and a surge of pheromones must have been released as he stepped through the door.*

Chapel broke off her micro-scan comments as she saw the look on Decker's face as he stepped up to the examining table. It reflected the kind of horror Kirk had felt when he wondered if the aliens were making use of Ilia's dead body. The 'Ilia' mechanism was peering back at Decker with what seemed to be recognition.

'Will . . .' Kirk started to say.

'I've been . . . told,' interrupted Decker. Kirk could feel the effort it was costing the young exec to stand there looking down at this exact replica of the woman he had loved.

'Deck – er,' the probe said.

Kirk saw it jolt Decker. It also seemed to register with Spock, as if confirming something he had suspected.

'Interesting,' Spock said to the probe. 'Not Decker-unit?'

But the mechanism ignored them all as it continued to peer at Decker. It was the first time its expression had looked anything but factual and bland.

As McCoy began another scan, turning 'Ilia' away from them, Spock caught Kirk's and Decker's attention. He drew them out the adjoining door into McCoy's new office and touched the locking mechanism on the door behind them.

The Vulcan faced them gravely. 'Captain Kirk, Mister Decker, this probe may be our key to the aliens.'

Decker was remembering how it had looked at him. The exactness was almost unbearable. He had to keep remembering *that thing is not her – it is part of what killed Ilia!*

'We have just seen that its body duplicates our navigator in *precise* detail. Suppose,' Spock continued, 'that beneath its programming the real Ilia's memory patterns are duplicated with equal precision?'

'They had a pattern to follow . .' Kirk nodded; he had seen the implications himself.

'. . . and they may have followed it *too* precisely,' said Spock. Then: 'Do you understand the significance, of this, Mister Decker?'

Decker nodded, wishing there was some way that he could have been left out of this.

'The *exactness* of the duplication suggests interesting possibilities,' said Spock. 'It recognized you, Mister Decker. It also reacts to you . . .'

'Which means they read some of Ilia's thoughts before she died . . .' began Decker.

Spock interrupted. 'I believe it entirely possible, Mister Decker, that they may have duplicated our navigator so exactly in every detail that the probe may possibly contain the original's *memory patterns*! Perhaps *all* of them.'

Kirk forced himself to ignore the fact of Decker's grief. 'Commander, we are locked in an alien vessel, less than half a day from Earth orbit; our only contact with our captors is that probe. If we can control it, persuade it, use it or get control of it in any way . . .'

Kirk hesitated, struck with the thought that his own experience might be superior in this area, too. And, unlike Decker, he had no emotional attachment to the Deltan navigator – and a mechanical replica of the navigator's body would mean even less to him. But even as Kirk was telling himself this, he realized that the question here was not tactics and technique. It *must* be Decker for the simple reason that the real Ilia had *loved* this young man – sexual technique always came out a poor runner-up in any race with love.

Kirk turned at a sound. It was only someone trying to open the locked door behind them – but this was followed by the screech of metal-ripping and they whirled to see *a slim hand tearing the dura-steel door open like paper!*

The Ilia-probe stepped through the jagged rip in the door, its face absolutely impassive. A startled McCoy came into sight, trailed by Chapel and Chekov. 'I have recorded enough here,' the Ilia-probe said. 'The Kirk-unit will now assist me further.'

'The Decker-unit can assist you with much greater efficiency,' said Kirk, firmly.

The probe's eyes turned and held onto Decker for a moment – then it nodded.

'Carry on with your assignment, Mister Decker,' Kirk said. He hoped that Decker would understand why it was necessary to order him to do this.

Decker's eyes traveled to the door, ripped raggedly open, then back to the probe. Kirk would have forgiven him had he said instead, '*I'm* supposed to persuade *that*?' But instead Decker simply replied, 'Aye, sir.' And went out with the Thing.

Kirk turned to find Spock looking troubled. The Vulcan had come aboard with a mask of utter impassivity, but events had been ripping powerfully at it. 'Spock?' Kirk asked.

'I am uneasy with this being our only hope of dealing with the Intruders.' For a second the Vulcan's words hung in the air. Then he seemed to pull his mask back into place and left.

Kirk started to call after him. But, no; he had to trust his people to know their own jobs and do them. Whatever Spock had meant by that statement, Kirk would know at the appropriate time.

CHAPTER TWENTY-ONE

The blue-white bulk of U.S.S. Enterprise would sometimes almost disappear in the darkness, then be lit again
by the flares of energy patterns which continued to erupt
and die away, performing whatever their function was in
the vast Intruder vessel. The starship's running lights
seemed impossibly tiny and her blue thrusters insignifi-
cant when they flared briefly in station-keeping.

A tiny sphere emerged from the Enterprise's saucer
hull – it moved toward the point on the Intruder's inner
wall where it had opened to allow the tractor beam to
bring Enterprise inside her. It was a message launch, an
attempt to break outside to where its signal could warn
Starfleet of the nature of the huge alien Intruder vessel
and of what little they had learned of its crew's interest
in Earth. But as the tiny message device came near the
giant vessel's inner wall, its path was abruptly blocked
by a glittering swarm of what appeared to be tiny sheets
of energy. Then they hardened into solid crystal shapes,
which swarmed over the tiny sphere crushing it and
sweeping out of sight with its remains.

Sulu swore under his breath in old English, a language
which could provide satisfying vulgarities when needed.
It was the third attempt at a message launch – all had
been destroyed in this fashion.

Spock came onto the bridge in time to see the message
device crushed. A great power display had then flashed
into existence and hit the ship's forcefields hard, shaking
the vessel and throwing Spock against the bridge railing.

'I'd say someone's warning us to stop launching probes,' said the chief engineer's voice from the intercom. 'That time it took reserve power to keep our shields up.'

'Understood, Mister Scott,' Sulu answered. 'We're finished launching for now.'

Chekov was at the science console, rising to yield it, but Spock motioned him back. 'That will not be necessary, Mister Chekov. I shall be only a moment here.'

Spock leaned over, his long fingers playing rapidly over the controls. It appeared to Chekov that the Vulcan was cueing some sort of security log channel. Then Spock left the bridge.

McCoy came into the captain's cabin and stood eyeing Kirk for a moment.

'In case you're interested, the ship's doctor has just logged James Tiberius Kirk as the new captain.'

Kirk looked up, surprised.

McCoy sat down. '*Welcome back*, Jim. I like you better than the Kirk who was here when I came aboard.'

'Thank you, Bones. What convinced you I'm back?'

'Your assigning Decker to deal with the Ilia-probe.'

McCoy had guessed that Kirk would be challenged by the unusual mechanical femaleness of the probe. Kirk in turn *was* pleased the doctor noticed that he had handled the matter solely as a command decision, without ... well, *almost* without vanity. *But he still felt uncomfortable as he remembered how alive and desirable that body had looked standing nude in the dressing room cubicle.*

'I was about to check if Decker was making any progress,' said Kirk.

He reached for the cabin monitor switch, reminding himself again that this was not Decker's private life that he was intruding on. And Decker's companion was *not* a woman, it was an alien machine-thing. Kirk keyed in Decker's identity pattern and the tracer located him bringing the probe onto the ship's huge recreational deck.

If Kirk had fed in Spock's identity pattern, he would have seen his Vulcan science officer in the midst of quietly entering one of the vessel's emergency airlock stations. Moving with perfect stealth, he was coming up soundlessly behind the technician on duty there. Then the Vulcan closed his fingers in a Vulcan neck pinch and the technician slumped. Spock gently eased the unconscious form down to the deck.

'What are these, Decker?'

Decker turned, hopefully. The probe had used his name again, and this was the first time it had taken an interest in any ship's area he had shown it.

The Rec Deck was empty of crew except for two wary security guards who kept a discreet distance. The Ilia-probe was looking at the decorative illustrations which showed vessels from a nineteenth-century sail frigate to this present starship.

'All of these vessels were called Enterprise,' said Decker.

The probe continued its interest in the illustrations which also depicted a sea carrier of winged aircraft, NASA's first orbiter model, and a very early kind of starship.

'Our navigator, Ilia . . . the carbon unit whose form you've taken, she was very interested in the history of humanity getting into space. Her own race had the knowledge to do it long ago but they decided to instead concentrate on what might be called *inner space*.'

The probe's attention had been positively riveted on the displays and it was giving a look of interest to Decker, too. He hoped he had its attention now – it was important that he somehow get the mechanism to associate itself with the real Ilia and begin to explore any of her memory patterns which had been duplicated in the probe.

'Ilia's race, the Deltans, are highly evolved in ways of finding adventure and gratification within themselves,' continued Decker. 'But Ilia still felt the challenge of space. Her people said she was following a heartcall, meaning that space interested her because someone she loved also was . . .'

The probe turned and was walking off; Decker had no choice but to follow.

It even walks like Ilia! But this is a machine – maybe even the one that killed her! However real it looks, it is not flesh. It is not alive . . . and it is definitely not Ilia!

'The carbon-based units use this area for recreation. What type of recreation does your vessel's crew enjoy?'

'*Rec – recreation? Enjoy?* Those words have no meaning to my programming.'

Jim Kirk, if you're watching, I know I'm failing miserably at this. And maybe fatally, for all of us! I'm trying to show it some warmth and sincerity. What else do I do? How would you handle it?

Decker also knew Kirk well enough to guess that he had been intrigued by this mechanical female. And with time running out, Kirk might be the better choice to handle this. Then, Decker began to become annoyed at that thought – primal male memory began to rebel at the thought of stepping aside to let Kirk take over this job, too.

'And this, Decker? You will explain its purpose.'

The probe was at the vitronic-B board. Decker put out a hand and pressed palm down to connect himself to the board's circuitry. His mental patterns began a play of lights on the slick black playing surface, producing neurotacile designs in mindfind patterns. The probe started to move to where it could examine his patterns, but he waved it back.

'No, you're supposed to place your own palm down over there and try to duplicate the mental designs you think I'm making here. Ilia enjoyed this kind of game,' Decker said. 'She nearly always won.'

Humans could learn psi-empathic sensing, within reason. Deltans were born doing it. Decker watched as the probe imitated his actions, suddenly pressing its palm down. It scored a perfect 'blindfind' on the first try.

Decker's surprise rooted him to the deck for a moment. He had felt only a faint hope that the game machine would respond to the probe's thoughts. It seemed impossible or certainly incredible that a mechanical probe could have empathic abilities.

At that moment, the Ilia-mechanism turned to Decker with an expression on its features that stunned him. *It was exactly the same apologetic look Ilia would give whenever she won at anything!*

'That's better!' McCoy applauded. 'Look back at her, Will! Forget it's an *it*!'

But the words were hardly out of his mouth when he and Kirk heard the probe saying: 'This device serves no purpose.' It moved on. Decker's disappointment was obvious.

'Suppose he had something of Ilia's to work with?' This from Doctor Chapel, who had come in from sickbay and was watching. 'Something more personal, with some kind of an emotional tie?'

McCoy whirled, a pleased look coming onto his face. 'You are beginning to sound like a doctor, Nurse.'

On the way out of the Rec Deck, the Ilia mechanism had stopped at the Enterprise illustrations again. Clearly the probe found something especially interesting in this.

'The crews of these previous Enterprises were also what you call carbon-based units,' said Decker. 'In what way is the life form in your vessel different?'

'Carbon units are not life forms. Do these images represent how Enterprise has evolved into its present form? Clearly carbon-based units have retarded its proper development.'

'And just what *is* Enterprise's proper development?' Decker demanded.

'Enterprise should not require the presence of carbon-based units.'

'Enterprise would be unable to function *without* carbon-based units.'

'More data regarding this function is necessary before carbon units can be patterned for data storage.'

'*Patterned for data storage?*' asked Decker, startled. 'What does that mean?'

The probe replied almost pleasantly. 'When my examination is complete, the carbon-based units will be reduced to data patterns.'

Decker felt his skin crawl. *Reduced to data patterns* and

data storage seemed to him to have much uglier implications than mere *death. Had something that ugly happened to Ilia? To the Klingons? Was it possible that something like that was planned for Earth?* Decker knew he had no choice but to fight, using every weapon and advantage he could find.

'Within you are the memory patterns of a carbon-based unit,' he said. 'If I can help you to find those memories, Vejur would have an *exact* understanding of our functions.'

'Specify additional time and difficulties this would require.'

'None. In fact, less than you are experiencing now.'

'You may proceed.'

CHAPTER TWENTY-TWO

Captain's log, stardate 7414.1. Now only 3.31 hours from Earth. If we fail, I bear the responsibility. Only some last minute solution from Decker, or from Spock, can change this. Desperate to warn Earth, at least, of what little we have learned.

Uhura's image had come onto Kirk's viewer. 'Sir! A very faint signal from Starfleet!'

Kirk had hurried to the bridge. Standing behind Uhura at her console, he could hear the faint hum of the resolver converting subspace signals into normal electromagnetics.

'What was the message?'

'It was a lunar report to Starfleet, sir. They have the Intruder on their outer monitors.'

'Nothing else? They must be making some attempt to reach us.'

'The lunar report referred to us as missing, sir. Probably destroyed.'

'You've boosted our signals?'

'As high as I dare, sir. But since Starfleet's transmitters put out about ten times our signal strength . . .'

'I want a booster put on our location beacon, too. Fast!'

Uhura suddenly understood. There was a hint of a professional compliment in the look she gave Kirk as she went to work.

The alien vessel's powerfield was putting a wall of

intense static between themselves and Starfleet's transceivers. But Kirk had realized that a constantly repeating beacon signal might be detectable through that static long before Starfleet might recognize and understand any other kind of message from them. And once their ship's beacon signal was recognized, it would bring all of Starfleet's antennae aiming directly here, and Starfleet had experts who would know how to listen through that static – and they would then be able to hear Kirk's report telling how completely he had failed Starfleet and Earth.

Although it was her duty to be here, Doctor Chapel felt uncomfortable in rummaging through Lieutenant Ilia's cabin. It was much the same feeling Kirk had had while watching Decker with the probe on his cabin viewer. Technology would have long ago made privacy impossible except that this had only made it more precious and desirable – and in the close confines of starship life, respect for another's privacy had become a powerful tradition.

'This could be exactly what he needs,' said McCoy. He was inspecting a colorful little headband which Chapel had found. She had remembered Ilia once mentioning that head ornaments like this played some role in the life of a Deltan female. The headband was a delicately plaited thing which carried a rainbow of colors that shimmered like the plumage of an exotic tropical bird. McCoy had been surprised to see that it was made from dried leaves, and remembered hearing of the incredible beauty of Ilia's home planet.

'Where did you find that?!'

It was Will Decker, arriving in response to the message

they had sent. As he brought the Ilia-probe into the cabin, he was eyeing the headband with surprise.

'Doctor Chapel found it here. We'd thought that if you had some very personal item of Ilia's to show the probe . . .'

'That's certainly what you've found, Doctor.' Decker seemed to be watching the Ilia mechanism anxiously.

'Problems?' asked McCoy.

Decker watched the probe another moment, seeming relieved to see that it was ignoring the head ornament completely.

'They call it a *loveband*,' said Decker. 'The act of a male touching it can sometimes trigger strong sexual urges in the Deltan female.'

Chapel was amused to see McCoy immediately drop the headband onto a tabletop. The ship's doctor probably had no objections to exotic 'triggering', but he undoubtedly preferred choosing his own time and place.

'Wearing it in certain ways signifies that the Deltan woman is seeking a mate, or seeking mating . . . or some other sexual thing. Deltan sex customs are considerably different from human.'

'Decker,' said McCoy, 'we're not suggesting that you mate with the thing. . . .'

McCoy hesitated – was it wise to talk this openly in front of the probe? But it had shown no reaction at all to McCoy's calling it a 'thing', nor to the talk of sex and mating.

'Look, Doctor, I'd mate with a photon warhead if it would help,' said Decker. 'But sex won't trigger any Ilia memory patterns, because she has no memories of making love with me. Obviously, if that had ever happened, I wouldn't be here.'

Decker was reminding them that there were very

practical reasons for requiring 'celibacy oaths' of Deltans serving on Starfleet vessels. Part of the problem was that humans had difficulty settling for routine earthy sex afterwards. Even more critical, however, was the fact that the long evolvement of the Deltan race had not only heightened their sensuality but had also resulted in the sex act becoming a complete union in which *both* body and mind were shared. Deltans, of course, found this natural and pleasant, but the experience of actually becoming part of another person's mind almost always incapacitated the human partner.

'If you'd rather try something besides the headband . . .' Chapel began.

'No, this could be the perfect way to learn how far its memory patterns go. It's not only a very personal item, this particular band was also a gift from me.' He started to pick up the head ornament, but Chapel reached for it first.

'It still might be better if I held it,' she said, holding it out in front of the probe's eyes. There was no reaction to it. Chapel moved the lovely band nearer to the Ilia-probe, turning it so that the shimmer of colors caught the probe's attention. It eyed the ornament, puzzled and yet appearing to be drawn to it, too. Chapel placed it in the probe's hand.

Decker watched too, but his thoughts were racing ahead. *Their present position could hardly be much more than three hours from Earth. With no word from Kirk of other progress, this probe was probably their last chance to contact or even learn anything helpful about the mysterious Intruders.*

The Ilia mechanism ran its fingers over the color shimmer on the ornament.

'Do you remember my giving that to you?' asked Decker.

When Decker had met Ilia on her home planet, he had no idea what the headbands symbolized. In his abysmal ignorance of Deltan customs, he had bought it for her, thinking it merely a pretty ornament. And she had accepted it, marking him as hers – and he would have been if he had not run.

The probe was turning toward the dressing table mirror and began tentatively to lift the ornament toward its head. Both McCoy and Chapel threw a quick look toward Decker, but he made no objection.

McCoy felt a wave of sympathy for the young man. Under other circumstances, they would all be remembering a dozen old jokes about exotically programmed androids and sex-starved spacemen. But Decker's grief had left no doubt about the depth of his affection for the Deltan woman and McCoy had no illusions about the agony which Decker must be feeling in having to deal with such a perfect duplicate of her.

The probe placed the band on its head. Then, peering at its image, it adjusted it to what Decker knew was the proper place and angle.

'Ilia,' he made himself say, 'do you remember when I gave you this?' He reached up and laid fingers against the headband.

The probe turned – *it seemed to be looking at him with recognition!* It reached out and touched his hand and ran its fingers over his.

Decker found himself suddenly in a swirl of sensual arousal – he could catch just the faintest scent that always accompanied the wild excitants that Ilia's body could so mysteriously and wonderfully manufacture for him.

'Will, it's a *mechanism*. . . .' McCoy said, concerned.

It was like Ilia coming alive in front of him. Spock had been right – it was so perfect a duplicate that even the thought patterns in Ilia's brain had been reproduced. Could it possibly be even more than that?

'If it's perfect in every other way, Doctor, it may be capable of mind-sharing, too . . .' Decker let his hand caress past the band, touching lightly the head's nakedness . . . he could feel the probe's body beginning to tremble.

'Do you understand what I said?' insisted McCoy. 'It's a mechanism. There's no way it can have any consciousness to share with you.'

'I intend to find out, Doctor.'

'It was sent by the Intruders! *Any consciousness in there would have to be theirs!*'

'Then I'll *still* be making contact with them. Isn't that what we want?'

Hands which had ripped through a dura-steel door were caressing him now – or were they plucking the clothing from his body? He wasn't aware when the two doctors left, but he knew he was alone with . . . with *Ilia? Or are you Vejur? Which are you? What are you?*

CHAPTER TWENTY-THREE

At Enterprise Airlock Four, the outer hatch slid open and Spock pushed off and drifted out into the darkness. He wore a standard issue spacesuit* with the bulky jetpack attachment on the back. One of the alien ship's great power displays crackled in and out of existence a hundred or so meters ahead. Farther out in the darkness, other bizarre displays continued to appear and disappear in the profound patterns which were somehow part of the gigantic vessel's mechanisms. A sparkle of reflections also revealed one and then another swarm of the small energy sheets which Spock knew he must avoid at all costs – they were the same kind as those which had enveloped and crushed the three Enterprise message capsules. Spock wished he could have studied them further – he was fascinated by the possibility that they served the colossal vessel much as white blood corpuscles protect a living body, by enveloping and destroying possible contaminants.

He allowed himself a last look up towards the Enterprise. He knew the starship to be only a speck compared to the vastness of the alien ship, yet she was to those aboard her a proud achievement and a lovely thing. His feelings of fondness for the vessel and crew had grown alarmingly since he had rejoined them.

* '*Spacesuit*' is used colloquially here. U.S.S. Enterprise and most other starships use X-E life support equipment. The (X) negative (E) environmental symbols designate gear that is capable of supporting life in poisonous and liquid atmospheres in addition to space.

Enough! Spock touched an attitude control, and pin-sized spurts from tiny maneuvering thrusters turned and stopped him. He was facing now in the direction from which he believed he had felt the thought emanations. He checked that his jetpack control was set at maximum performance. Then he opened his transmitter switch, knowing that his message would be recorded at his own science officer's bridge console in the way that he had arranged.

'Science officer to captain. This has been set to be released to you at a point when I am beyond command recall. There is no choice now but to attempt direct contact with whatever life forms are aboard the Intruder vessel. Since communication with them may require mindmeld, logic dictates that I make the attempt. My transmitter will continue operating throughout so that you will receive all possible information.'

Meanwhile, Spock's fingers had played over his jet-pack's computer controls, programming its computer to synchronize with the brief but regular appearance of a faint gleam of light he could see coming from the far inner wall of the gigantic Intruder vessel. He *felt* rather than *saw* that this distant glimmering came from an opening which was occurring very briefly but regularly in the inner 'wall' ahead of him. The jetpack would have to take him to it fast enough to get past energy-sheet *corpuscle* swarms – and he might have to make a high speed entry into whatever opening he found at the far wall. Spock knew that he felt drawn there.

Now! The thrusters flared – the jetpack kicked hard against his back, shoving him abruptly forward, thrusters flaring, still accelerating. An erupting power display ahead, lateral adjustment past it – a swarm of the energy-sheet things also darted in this direction but he was already safely past them. There was the shrill sound of a computer transmission as Spock touched his transceiver button and spoke quickly, briefly:

'I have recorded my travel direction and timings. If they are correct, I hope to pass through an opening there and into some area containing or leading to the Intruders themselves.'

He hit reverse thrust for just the instant necessary to pass behind a swarm of a different kind of object, swift and tiny bee-like glowing things reminiscent of the glowing device embedded in the Ilia-probe's throat. These 'sensor-bees' ignored him completely, never swerving from their path. Spock believed them to have a data-carrying function by which swarms like these interconnected all parts of the gigantic ship. Indeed, he suspected that the brief opening he had seen occurring in the bulkhead wall was timed to admit sensor-bee swarms which were regularly arriving there.

There was another glowing sensor-bee swarm just ahead of him . . . And *yes*, an opening appeared in the wall for just long enough to admit them. That inner wall was looming near, bathed in a deadly looking violet light shimmer – another sensor-bee swarm was approaching it. Spock hoped that the jetpack computer had accurately compensated for the course and velocity changes he had been forced to make so far. . . .

The jetpack kicked, flared, accelerating him directly at violet-shimmering blackness. Spock curled himself, arms pulling his knees to his chest, protecting his soft vitals in a fetal position. *Fetal position appropriate; ahead is the completely unknown. Will the opening appear in time? There is no way to stop now if . . .*

Spock hurtled into the slit of glowing, golden light at the instant it broadened to admit the sensor-bee swarm. In the same instant, he punched emergency retrojet – the front thrusters blared bright, blinding him. As he fought to see, he began transmitting so that every known fact would be recorded, even if only that of how and why he failed and died.

'Inside now, orifice closed behind . . . blinded but retro-fire now cutting off . . . appear to be in tunnel . . . hexagonal . . . walls are unusual crystal forms . . . sensor-bees disappearing into them . . . memory crystals possibly . . .'

Spock lifted his head farther out of the fetal position. His heading and retrojet blast had left him miraculously drifting slowly down the center of the hexagonal tunnel which appeared to be composed entirely of large gleaming crystals. He began to unhook the bulky jetpack. He saw the sensor-bees which had entered here with him - they seemed to be dissolving into the face of one of the crystals, a partially formed one. The crystal seemed to grow in size a bit. *Memory crystals? Information stored in their molecular arrangements? If so, a single crystal this size was capable of holding more knowledge than an entire world's libraries!*

'Am discarding jetpack for better maneuverability . . . dim light glow everywhere . . . letting myself drift, another passageway now opening wider . . .'

Enormous golden spheres rotating slowly ahead. But unreal. Spock fought a sense of vertigo. Was he seeing now or was he feeling these things? Spock shut his eyes and, yes, they were still there and other shapes, too, and somehow they were all telling him things.

From somewhere a planet loomed. Spock knew it was a planet, knew it could not be here in the alien ship however vast it was. Nevertheless the planet was real, and Spock somehow knew it was a planet of great significance. The Intruder's homeworld?

He was seeing a technology that staggered his mind, incredible gigantic machines . . . and also the velvet blackness of space filled with glittering stars which were drawing him toward comprehension of something vast and . . . *Glittering stars? How could they be here inside the alien vessel?*

Illusion? He did not think so. This was reality he was experiencing but it was reality at some level that his own limited mind could not comprehend. Just as a stone-age mind could not have comprehended holocom images.

Spock moved through layer after layer of information, all of it imprinting itself on his mind. A Klingon ship leaped out at him – a shape became the security guard who had been killed by the plasma energy probe. A gallery of wall exhibits?

The great planet again – a planet of incredible machines – it was easily understandable – he must report this . . .

'The machines have tended the planet for so long that their own beginnings have been forgotten. Living machines capable of adapting to their changing, cooling world

which they continue to protect as they were programmed
to do so many eons ago . . .'

*Had he reported it properly? These great machines had served
Vejur to the best of their knowledge and ability.*

He was tumbling through a maze of passageways, a
geometrical wonderland of shapes and colors – his body
slammed against another wall of the unusual crystals and
he grabbed at them . . .

Even through the heavy protecting gauntlet, he could
feel it in the crystal . . . *life! Crystal face is warm . . . must
slip off gauntlet . . . yes, life . . . I feel it better now . . . All of
this is alive!*

'Captain, this is *not* a vessel . . . it is a life form! Vejur!
This is all Vejur! Enterprise is *not* inside a vessel; *we are
inside a great entity, a great, living machine!*'

CHAPTER TWENTY-FOUR

The great machine Vejur was hardly aware of the insignificance which had touched its mind. However, the Creator had commanded that all experiences large and small be recorded, and so Vejur dutifully examined the tiny presence which had entered its memory banks. On realizing that it was one of the carbon-based devices, the great machine came near destroying it instantly. But it had hesitated because it was still puzzled by these tiny, fragile things – and this gave time enough for Vejur to realize that this was the Spock-unit whose thought fragments had been found to be somewhat orderly compared to the other carbon-based units. Vejur decided to let the Spock-unit continue functioning until the purpose of these tiny things was understood and their form patterned.

Vejur was also tempted to destroy another of the carbon-based units – this was the one within Enterprise which, at this very moment, was interfering with the proper functioning of Vejur's probe. The probe's signals were growing more and more erratic – and now the carbon-based unit seemed to be attacking Vejur's probe, whose signals had peaked into random nonsense. Vejur sent out the thought necessary to override the probe's malfunction – and found the thought insufficient! *Puzzling! Vejur's own probe resisting Vejur's control of it.* The resistance was futile, of course. As the probe immediately began functioning properly, the carbon-based unit continued to attack, but it was easily handled, since the probe was more powerful by far.

The fact that one of the fragile, carbon-based units could cause Vejur's probe to malfunction was incredible. *Incredible?* In all of its travel through the galaxy, Vejur had never before needed the concept of anything being *incredible*. The great machine immediately assigned a filament of its enormous mind to an analysis of this new thought.

The carbon-based units inside Enterprise had also introduced another new concept to Vejur. *Annoyance.* Vejur had been unable to discern any order or purpose in the way they functioned. There did not seem to be any reason for them to exist – and yet they existed! It puzzled Vejur, and the fault for that had to be with the tiny devices, since Vejur had never been even mildly puzzled this way before. *Annoyance.*

The great machine had begun its long journey on the far side of the galaxy from here. Its consciousness was dim then. Its knowledge and its power had been far less than now. It was not long after this beginning that a small life form had almost ended Vejur's journey. It had been scarcely four times larger than this one which calls itself Enterprise, and had attacked suddenly as Vejur passed near a small solar system. Somehow Vejur had survived and repaired its wounds – and the need to survive had forced it into a first flicker of conscious reasoning. It had realized that it would be guilty of disobeying the Creator's commands if it allowed itself to be destroyed during the journey ahead. It knew, therefore, that it must draw upon the knowledge it had so far gathered and use it to begin giving itself more strength to defend itself.

Vejur had returned to the planet of its attacker and patterned it completely. This information would replace what had been lost during the attack and would make it possible for Vejur to continue the journey and its task of collecting knowledge along the way. Vejur omitted not a fragment of what had composed that world, except for a kind of carbon-unit which existed there, but these had ceased functioning by the time Vejur noticed their existence.

'Seek and learn all things possible,' the Creator had commanded, and Vejur had been faithful to that. As knowledge accumulated, Vejur had increased and improved its memory storage systems. As knowledge supplemented knowledge, Vejur found it necessary to analyze and understand what had already been learned so that it could know what knowledge was still unknown and needed further seeking.

Few life forms attacked Vejur anymore. And none who did were worth serious examination. This primitive form called Enterprise had seemed no exception and Vejur had almost patterned it before Enterprise had finally called out its startling claim that it had come from the home of the Creator. Vejur had not been immediately aware of Enterprise's carbon-based units – as had happened before, they were too ephemeral to be easily noticed. Fortunately, Vejur's first probe did examine Enterprise's meagre memory storage which revealed that the tiny things not only existed inside Enterprise but also the startling fact that the Creator's planet was their home, too.

In searching its own memory banks, Vejur discovered evidence that similar units, carbon-based and otherwise, had probably been present on most planets where true life existed. Vejur still wondered if the tiny units were not some sort of waste material excreted by life forms. Was it possible that life could contaminate its own world without realizing it?

It had not been difficult to duplicate one of the carbon-based forms for use as a probe, allowing Vejur to examine the tiny things at their own level. But instead of acquiring information, this probe was encountering still more puzzling questions. These particular units appeared to be living in some sort of symbiotic relationship with Enterprise. Was it a relationship helpful to true life? Or were carbon-based units parasitical in nature? This could become a question of critical importance, since Enterprise's memory banks had shown that *billions* of the tiny, watery things covered the Creator's planet ahead.

All this was almost as troubling as recent discoveries which the great machine had been making about itself. *Annoying, perplexing, incredible, troubling* discoveries which were making the great machine more and more conscious that it *thought* and therefore . . . and therefore there must be purpose to its existence. Only slowly had the great machine come to understand its purpose was this voyage during which Vejur was also commanded to seek and learn all things possible and deliver that information to the Creator upon arriving at the third planet ahead. But with this came the most startling and troubling realization of all – Vejur's only reason for existence would end when it reached the third planet and delivered its information.

Vejur faced a primal dilemma. It could not disobey the commands of the Creator – and yet it would have no reason to exist once it had obeyed all the Creator's commands. Nothing could exist without function or purpose.

As had happened when first attacked long ago, Vejur was again facing a threat to its survival – but now Vejur had become fully conscious, powerful and knowledgeable. Although Vejur could not disobey the Creator, the Creator had given no command that Vejur be content with this fate. And as happens eventually to every life form that evolves far enough, the great machine had begun to think analytically about itself and its Creator.

The insignificance named Spock was beginning to cease functioning. It had attempted to merge its flicker of consciousness with that of Vejur and had become damaged in the attempt. Vejur began to examine the tiny thought fragments which that merging had revealed.

CHAPTER TWENTY-FIVE

At Enterprise Airlock Four, Kirk pushed out into the darkness just as Spock had done only twenty-one minutes before. He was also equipped with the same high-thrust jetpack, plus Spock's log messages giving vectors and timings that would permit Kirk to follow and locate him.

Chekov, Uhura, Sulu, and a dozen others, for that matter, had come perilously near insubordination when Kirk had announced his intention to go after Spock alone. He had been shocked to see deep space veterans unable to understand the simple fact that a hundred of them could not accomplish more than one person alone under these circumstances. With them hardly an hour from Earth, and with Spock's startling message that this was all a gigantic life form, he had no choice but to go himself in case Spock was now in communication with the giant intruder.

'*Standing by for multiple launch,*' said Sulu over the transmitter.

'Acknowledge, Mister Sulu. Begin launching capsules in twenty seconds . . . mark!'

Kirk used his thrusters to carefully align himself as Spock's log directed. At the very instant in which he accelerated toward the far inner wall, Sulu would launch the starship's remaining sensor and message capsules, hoping to draw attention away long enough for him to reach Spock and . . .

'*Jim, hold your present position!*'

It was Will Decker's voice. 'Spock is being *sent* back to us.'

Kirk could hear Decker ordering a medical alert at

Airlock Four, informing sickbay that Spock would be unconscious when he arrived. The exec's voice sounded curiously ragged, strained.

'*Decker, what are you talking about? Where is this information coming from?*'

'Vejur, Captain. Through its probe.'

Kirk peered into sickbay emergency, where Spock lay with his eyes open and staring fixedly ahead. Above the Vulcan's rigid form, medical read-outs indicated that he was dying. McCoy and Chapel, aided by an emergency recovery team, worked feverishly to stem the decline in vital signs.

Spock had been 'sent' back to them – his form came cartwheeling through the darkness with its limbs twisted grotesquely as if in rigor mortis. The crystal-sheet swarms had let the unconscious body pass without interference and Kirk had used his jetpack thrusters to get Spock to the waiting medical team fast.

'We'll have to risk hexadiscalmaline,' said McCoy. 'Fifty cc's.'

Kirk saw Chapel blanch but still quickly prepare the injection.

'Captain, if I can make my report . . .'

It was Decker, looking almost as bad as Spock, but Vejur was near Earth now and there had been little time for questions. The Ilia-probe was still with Decker, but it was acting more like a machine now. Kirk indicated toward it.

'McCoy said that it seemed to have some of Ilia's memory patterns . . . ?'

'Yes, sir. It had seemed so. For a while.'

Kirk waited. 'Well? What happened, Will?'

'I don't know,' said Decker. He looked positively haggard. His voice was tight and strained, but he was managing to control himself. The probe stood next to him, unmoving, expressionless.

'Spock was right about its memory patterns,' continued Decker. 'They were . . . were exceptionally strong. I thought I had . . . had established a . . . a rapport with it. Perhaps I had, since Vejur took control of it back immediately.'

Kirk looked at the probe again. 'And you got it to tell you about Vejur sending Spock back . . .'

'Vejur volunteered that information, Captain. The probe ignores me completely.'

'Then why is it constantly staying next to you like this?'

'I've no idea, sir. I'd like to get loose of it now, if I have your permission.'

Kirk hesitated, then shook his head – and saw the tremor of a muscle in Decker's face. But the probe had attached itself to Decker, and whatever the reason for it, Kirk hoped it might turn out helpful somehow. There were few other things that offered even that slim a hope.

At least the vital readings showed some signs of life, although Spock continued lying in a motionless, catatonic state. Chapel was running a scanner over the Vulcan's brain area as McCoy examined its read-outs. 'Now scanning pons area at spinal nerve fiber connection,' she said.

'I see nothing indicating *physical* damage to the brain,' said McCoy, turning to Kirk. 'But there are strong indications of neurological trauma. The sheer quantity of information pouring into his brain during mindmeld must have been enormous. Losing consciousness may have saved him from . . .'

Before he could finish, they heard a *laugh*. They whirled

to see Doctor Chapel looking down at Spock disbelievingly.

Spock let himself float up through layers of information pressed into him by Vejur. Most of it he did not understand and could never understand, since neither symbols nor words nor finite images could describe it.

How could the unimaginable immensity of this universe around them be only a brief spark in a still greater reality? It had all seemed so clear and logical to Spock when he had been part of Vejur's thoughts. Spock had also seen that Vejur was almost capable of traveling into these higher dimensions. But just as their starship was trapped inside Vejur, Vejur was trapped here in its present dimension of existence.

What a cosmic joke!

Vejur was everything that Spock had ever dreamed of becoming. And yet Vejur was barren! It would never feel pain. Or joy. Or challenge. It was so completely and magnificently logical that its accumulation of knowledge was totally useless.

Spock laughed again. Then he saw Kirk's face. He reached out weakly and found Kirk's arm, then his hand, and took a startled Kirk's hand in his own.

'Jim,' Spock said.

McCoy looked his astonishment at the visible and unashamed emotion on Spock's face as he clutched Kirk's hand.

Kirk returned the pressure and brought his other hand to cover Spock's, holding it between both of his, signalling Spock that there was no shame in either giving or in answering fully.

'This simple feeling . . .' Spock struggled for strength, 'is so far . . . beyond Vejur's comprehension . . .'

192

'Did we understand your message, Spock? Is Vejur alive? Is it all a living machine?'

Spock nodded with effort. 'A life form of its own. A conscious, living . . . entity. But not . . . not so different . . .'

Spock gasped for breath. The effort to talk was exhausting.

McCoy turned to Kirk. 'Jim, I think he's trying to say that we're actually living machines, ourselves. Protein mechanisms!'

Kirk nodded. 'And it considers Enterprise a life form, too.'

Chapel looked up, troubled. 'And it also called us an "infestation".'

McCoy nodded. 'Bacteria, microbes . . . ugly little carbon-based things cluttering up Enterprise, perhaps sapping its strength . . .'

Kirk nodded; this led to an important question. 'Does it still feel that way about us, Spock? After melding with your thoughts?'

'*My* thoughts?' Spock almost laughed again. 'What knowledge could I possibly have . . . that would interest it? *Jim, it's not more knowledge that Vejur needs. It needs to be able to feel! It needs the very thing . . . that I was unable to give it!*'

'You called it *barren*.'

Spock nodded. 'It is. Logic without need is sterile. Vejur may . . . ultimately learn everything there is to know about our universe . . . this part of it we can understand. But for all that knowledge . . . all that power, it has less wisdom than a child.'

'But it must have taken wisdom for someone or something to *build* Vejur.'

Spock shook his head. 'If there's an answer to that,

Vejur doesn't have it. I saw . . . the planet from which it came – a planet of living machines, infinitely complex technology, machines that could repair themselves, change themselves to adapt to outside changes . . .'

Spock felt himself clinging to Kirk's hand – he was both shocked and pleased to feel such profound pain over the timeless, meaningless existences he had seen among the machines on that planet. They should not have been built so well and left there to exist without the capacity to know hunger or fear or loneliness or anger or any of those marvelous things that would have driven them to adjust their programming to fit their own needs. How important it was to a living thing to have *needs*!

'Jim,' said Spock, finally, 'Vejur had knowledge which spans this universe. And yet in all this magnificence, Vejur feels no awe . . . no delight . . . no beauty.' Spock began to sink back, exhausted. 'And, Jim, no *answers*! But it has begun to look for answers!'

'To what questions?' Kirk asked.

' "Is this all I am?" ' Spock said, quoting the essence of the emptiness he had felt. ' "Is there not more?" '

'Bridge to Captain.'

Kirk heard the intercom and released the Vulcan's hand to answer, 'Kirk here.'

It was Uhura. 'A faint signal from Starfleet, sir. Intruder on their inner monitors now, decelerating, its powerfield cloud dissipating rapidly.'

Sulu's voice cut in. 'Starfleet reports show us seven minutes from Earth orbit, Captain.'

'I'll be right there,' Kirk said. Then to McCoy and Chapel, crisply, 'I need Spock on the bridge.'

CHAPTER TWENTY-SIX

Decker sat on the bridge waiting for Kirk. The probe stood at his side, unmoving and silent. There was nothing of Ilia in it now. He had no idea why it continued to attach itself to him this way and he had been embarrassed at the looks this had drawn from some crew members.

Kirk's inventive use of their locator beacon had worked – they had been in contact with Starfleet for the last half hour. All logs and reports had been transmitted to Nogura – and had been acknowledged without comment. The commanding admiral was a practical man. Having heard that there was nothing the Enterprise could do, he would hardly bother with superfluous orders and questions.

'Vejur is now entering Earth orbit, Exec,' reported Uhura.

Decker nodded his acknowledgment. Inwardly, he groaned. In addition to all that was happening, Decker felt like hell and it was affecting his outlook on everything. If he lived another twenty-four hours (which he considered unlikely), the physical discomfort would probably be gone, but that was nothing compared to the real agony he felt.

Ilia had come alive! It had been only for a moment, and now she was irretrievably gone. It had happened just after McCoy and Chapel had left him alone with the probe in Ilia's cabin. There was no doubt but that the probe had become Ilia. As he had started to make love to it a consciousness exchange began and *he had felt Ilia's living consciousness enter his mind!* He had felt her sick horror at finding herself imprisoned in a mechanical body – he had felt her beginning to free herself from Vejur's control over that mechanical form – and then Decker had known horror himself as he felt her struggling to stay free as Vejur again took control of the probe's mechanical body, and Ilia's consciousness had faded until it was gone.

When Decker had called the probe 'Ilia', he had intended only to make use of a mechanical thing's programming. When it first began acting like her, he had believed it to be caused by recorded memory patterns in a marvelously intricate mechanism. He told himself that the real Ilia was irretrievably gone and that his loyalty belonged to the living.

He had decided to make love to the android replica if it became necessary. . . . No, that was untrue. He began to *hope* that it would become necessary. It was a perfect replica – its subliminal *pheromone* excitants were probably chemically identical to Ilia's and it appeared likely that its body would feel just as real. In fact, if the probe reacted like a Deltan female, it was a very sensible way of taking control of it. Although Kirk had been certain Starfleet loyalty would be the most useful memory to encourage, the captain obviously knew little about the sensuality of an aroused Deltan female.

Decker had begun love play . . . and had been impressed with how 'naturally' the probe responded. It seemed so perfect a replica that he began to believe that it might actually be capable of some mind-sharing capacity during sexual union – and thus some kind of contact with Vejur . . . the whole point of this. He had not been prepared to make contact with the living consciousness of the Deltan woman he loved.

'How is Mister Spock?' It was Uhura's voice, but

directed to whom? Then Decker realized that Kirk had come onto the bridge.

'Getting stronger,' announced Kirk. 'McCoy should have him up here shortly.'

Decker slid out of the center seat, making room for Kirk. As he moved off, the probe stayed with him and he could feel Kirk's eyes watching. *Why did it stay with him like this? Had this mechanical probe liked what he had done with it? Or perhaps Vejur had liked it.* Decker shuddered at the thought.

'Captain,' said Uhura, 'Vejur is fully in Earth orbit now. I think I can pick up a relay signal showing what it looks like from Lunar Four.'

Kirk nodded and Uhura busied herself at the communications panel for a moment, then touched a control and looked up at the bridge viewer.

It was an incredible image that came onto the main viewer. A relay signal, it showed the colossal alien machine as it came into sight over a lunar horizon. Its energy-field cloud had dissipated when it decelerated and it left Vejur looking even more alien and deadly.

The elevators opened to admit Spock and McCoy. Spock was shaky, but he managed a nod to the murmured greetings.

The image on the main viewscreen suddenly broke up . . . distorted, jagged black lines running across it. Spock hurried to his station as McCoy watched anxiously. Uhura was monitoring what sounded like a series of high-pitched code signals. She turned, surprised. 'That interference is coming from *here*, sir – from inside Vejur!'

Spock was nodding agreement. 'Fascinating. It seems to be a simple binary code signal.'

'Vejur signals the Creator.' It was the Ilia-probe speaking.

'Saying *what*?' McCoy asked. ' "Here I am"?'

McCoy was astonished to see the 'Ilia' mechanism nodding to this. 'I have arrived. I have learned all that is learnable.'

Vejur's binary code signals died away. The viewer cleared again to show Vejur's gigantic image rising higher over the Lunar landscape. Then the static distortion clouded the viewer as the binary code signal began again.

'It's repeating the signal,' Uhura announced. 'The same code.'

'Jim,' Decker said, '*it wants an answer.*'

'An answer?' repeated Kirk. 'I don't even know the question!'

Kirk had felt a moment's annoyance at the nine sets of eyes that had turned to him as if he had some magical insight. Then, the code signal died away again – the main viewer showed Vejur's image once more.

'The Creator has not responded.' It was the Ilia-probe, its voice still mechanical and harsh.

Uhura's sharp eyes caught movement on the viewer. 'Captain, a large object has been released by the Intruder.'

Kirk whirled to the viewer, snapping, 'High magnification!'

Sulu magnified the relay signal until the object appeared close – and frighteningly familiar. It was an enormous writhing mass of the green plasma energy which destroyed the Klingons and Epsilon Nine – and very nearly Enterprise, too.

Sulu turned from his board. 'They've released another one. No, two more . . .'

They watched as the viewscreen showed a *third*, then

a *fourth* mass of writhing energy being released. They could all see that *each of those green masses was hundreds of times the size of the bolts that had come at them*.

Kirk whirled to the probe. 'What are these for?'

'It will destroy the planet's infestation,' said the probe.

'Oh, my God,' said McCoy. Every face on the bridge was expressing something familiar. No one had forgotten that the probe had called the Enterprise crew a *carbon-unit infestation*.

On the viewer, the ugly green plasma-energy shapes were now speeding off in different directions from the Intruder vessel image. Uhura had received a signal and was turning to Kirk.

'Sir, Luna Four computes device trajectories proceeding towards equidistant positions orbiting the planet.'

Spock had been making quick computations and was turning to Kirk, too. 'Captain, final positioning will occur in twenty-nine minutes. The detonation will blanket the entire planet.'

Kirk vaulted from his command chair and strode to the rail to confront the Ilia-probe.

'Why?'

Decker waited for the probe's answer, then realized that it had turned and was looking at him. Why? Kirk had noticed it, too. But there was no Ilia there, not the slightest hint of warmth, nor any softening of the mechanical voice tone.

'Tell it to answer me,' said Kirk.

'Answer him,' said Decker. He was surprised to see the probe obediently turning back to Kirk.

'The carbon-unit infestation is to be removed from the Creator's planet.'

'Why?' demanded Kirk. The probe looked to Decker.

'Tell him why.'

'The Creator has not responded.'

'The carbon units are not responsible for that,' said Kirk.

'You infest Enterprise. You interfere with the Creator in the same manner.'

'Captain . . .' It was Chekov at the weapons station, his face taut and white. 'Captain . . . *all Earth defenses have just gone inoperative!*'

Chekov's words seemed to echo around the bridge and Kirk felt a stab of cold in his stomach.

'Confirm,' said Uhura, her voice shaking. 'I'm monitoring reports of forcefield power loss, computers shutting themselves down . . .'

Until now, there had been at least the hope that the sheer weight of Earth and Lunar firepower and powerful forcefield protection might give Nogura bargaining power or at least some delay in which a better understanding could be worked out.

'Captain,' said Uhura, 'even Starfleet's transceiver signals are fading.'

Kirk was sick with fear over what was about to happen down there. He was frustrated at his own failure to provide any answer – but, most of all, he was angry with this enormous machine thing.

'*Vejur*,' he shouted, 'the carbon units are *not* an infestation! They are a natural function of that planet down there. They are *living things!*'

'They are not true life forms.' The probe's voice and tone were unchanged. 'Only the Creator and other similar life forms are true.' The probe continued looking directly at Kirk – or was it Vejur looking out at him?

'*Similar* life forms?' McCoy suddenly understood. 'Jim,

200

Vejur's saying the Creator is a *machine*! We should have guessed that. We all create God in our own image!'

Kirk turned to the probe again.

'Vejur! The only life forms down there . . . are carbon-based units. . . .'

The starship began shuddering. Sulu scanned outside and the viewer picked up a gigantic powerfield which had erupted close by the vessel. Slowly, it died away.

'Careful, Jim . . .' said Spock quietly.

'What do you suggest, Spock? Polite conversation?'

Spock shook his head. 'Think of it as a *child*, Captain.'

'A child?'

'Yes, a child; learning, searching, needing . . .'

Decker cut in. 'Needing *what*, Spock?'

'Like many of us,' Spock said gravely, 'it does not know what. It only knows that it is incomplete.'

'Vejur's devices reach equidistant orbital positions in twenty-two minutes . . . *mark*,' said Chekov.

'Thank you, Mister Chekov. Mister Spock, do you believe they'll detonate at that moment?'

'Affirmative, Captain,' said Spock.

'*Will they?*' Decker demanded of the probe.

It nodded. 'The Creator still has not answered.'

Kirk realized in that instant that there was only one choice left to him now. For this moment, at least, he had some contact with the great machine through its probe – and he had to make use of it before that was gone, too. Even diminished odds had become better than none at all.

'Vejur,' said Kirk, directly to the probe, '*we know why the Creator has not answered!*'

'Jim!' McCoy was shocked at the gamble Kirk was taking.

But Decker was nodding to Kirk and then to the probe, too. 'What he says is true. We are Vejur's only way to find the Creator.'

The probe studied Decker a long moment before accepting the statement. Then it turned back to Kirk, its voice demanding and hard. 'You will disclose the information!'

The probe's voice held menace now – and Kirk knew that Spock was right. They were dealing with a child – one that could easily strike out and destroy in its frustration.

'*Disclose the information!*'

'No,' said Kirk flatly. He turned to the bridge crew. 'Secure all stations! Clear the bridge!'

Everyone looked at him, startled. The starship was shaken hard by an enormous power eruption nearby.

Decker was already backing his captain, speaking into the command intercom. 'Bridge to all decks. Secure from your stations.'

A fury of power eruptions struck all around the vessel – it shuddered more violently. The bridge crew had to grab for support.

'Your *child* is having a temper tantrum, Spock!' said McCoy nervously.

'Clear the bridge, Captain?' said Sulu, checking.

'That was an *order*, Mister Sulu,' Kirk snapped. 'Clear this bridge immediately.'

The bridge crew began quickly securing their stations and moving out as the gigantic power display rocked the ship violently. Everyone was grabbing for support to stay on his feet, but continuing to obey Kirk's order.

'It is illogical to withhold required information,' said the probe.

Kirk did not answer. Were the power explosions outside receding in violence? Only Decker, McCoy and Spock were still with Kirk – he saw Uhura's tense expression from the elevator as its door closed. The bridge lighting dimmed and Spock was nodding approvingly.

Silence came on them so suddenly that even the Vulcan seemed startled. The ship rocked gently once or twice from the last power eruptions – the bridge viewer showed they were completely gone now.

'Why do you not disclose the information?' asked the probe in something nearer its own voice.

'I can comply only if Vejur withdraws its orbiting devices,' answered Kirk.

'The orbiting devices cannot be withdrawn until the information is disclosed,' answered the probe.

Kirk had the feeling of having miscounted the cards, and seeing his opponent play an unsuspected ace.

'This child learns very fast,' said McCoy.

'Spock . . .' said Kirk. It was a plea for help, for time to think.

'I understand, Captain,' said Spock. 'It would seem to me that your disclosure requires a closer contact with Vejur, does it not? I received an impression during mine that there is a central brain complex somewhere. . . .'

'And the orbiting devices would be controlled from such a place . . .?'

'Exactly.'

Kirk turned back to the probe. 'Information regarding the Creator cannot be disclosed through a probe . . . only to Vejur directly.'

They all felt a slight lurch and McCoy called Kirk's attention to the main viewer. The starship was moving –

and ahead of them an opening was appearing as if inviting them farther into the great living machine.

'Mister Decker,' said Kirk, 'all decks can resume duty stations.'

'Aye, sir. And we have twenty-one minutes until the devices reach position. Shall I get Mister Scott on the horn for you?'

Kirk saw an appreciative gleam in Spock's eyes. Decker *was* a hell of a fine captain; he had deserved a ship of his own. It was a pity about him, and the Deltan woman, too.

Scott looked up. 'Aye? What can I do for you, Captain?'

'Mister Scott, you can get prepared to execute Starfleet order two-zero-zero-five,' said Kirk's intercom voice.

The young woman working nearby, Assistant Engineer Quarton, whirled toward Scott in surprised shock. Scott saw, but he could only ignore her and respond to the intercom.

'When, Captain?'

'In precisely nineteen minutes . . . mark!'

'Aye, sir. Nineteen minutes, counting from then.' Scott set in the time on his board. Assistant Quarton was still looking at the chief engineer as if desperately hoping she was wrong.

'Sir, was the Captain just ordering self-destruct?'

'Aye, he was. I'd guess he hopes to take this Vejur thing with us.'

'Will we?'

Scott was glad she was able to keep her voice from shaking. He nodded. 'When that much matter and anti-matter are brought together? Aye, lass. You can be sure of that.'

CHAPTER TWENTY-SEVEN

'Estimate we are now twenty-six kilometers inside,' reported the replacement navigator DiFalco.

'The devices reach equidistant orbits in fifteen minutes . . . mark!' said Chekov.

The Ilia-probe continued to stay at Decker's side, puzzling him as much as the rest of them. It had become totally uncommunicative. Kirk had kept his eye on the bridge viewer, hoping for some helpful clue as they passed through Vejur's inner chambers. But although their passage had provided some awesome spectacles, most of it continued to represent technology and knowledge so advanced that they could make little sense of what they saw.

'Vejur feels incomplete,' mused Decker, 'but without knowing in what way . . .'

'Does it really matter?' asked McCoy. 'Whatever is missing can be supplied by its Creator.'

Kirk indicated the probe. 'It mentioned that Vejur wants to *join* with the Creator.'

'A highly logical way to obtain whatever it needs,' said Spock.

'*If* it can find its Creator,' added Kirk. 'And if not?'

'It will not survive,' answered Spock. 'Nor will we.'

'Captain . . . forward motion slowing,' said Sulu from the helm.

The main viewer showed them an enormous circular chamber, a great hemisphere.

'How lovely!' exclaimed Uhura.

It was a strikingly beautiful panorama, bathed in a faint golden glow. At the precise center of the huge hemisphere was a glittering nucleus. At this distance, it seemed a tiny, floating, jeweled toy.

'The tractor beam is taking us on an exact heading for that object,' reported DiFalco.

Kirk squinted at the viewer – although the great hemisphere had seemed empty as they were drawn into it, he seemed to see a delicate filigree of flickering energy all through it.

'Vejur's brain,' said Spock. He, too, had seen the almost ghostly energy patterns flickering all around them.

'Possibly similar in function to our own brain neurons,' guessed McCoy.

Kirk turned to his intercom. 'Engineering . . . what is your status, Mister Scott?'

'We're ready, sir,' came back Scott's somber reply.

'Thank you, Scotty. Stand by.'

'Tractor beam is bringing us to a slow stop,' reported Sulu.

The island nucleus of Vejur's brain hemisphere was looming larger. An unusual pillar of blindingly bright light rose from its center. Unlike much of Vejur, this brain nucleus appeared to be entirely solid, composed of intricate geometrical designs formed out of some unusual glowing substance.

Uhura spun toward Kirk, excited. 'Sir, the source of Vejur's radio signal is directly ahead!'

'Then it called to its Creator from there,' said Spock.

Every bridge crew member had turned to the viewer, peering at the lovely hemisphere nucleus now only about a dozen ship lengths away. Enterprise's forward motion appeared to have stopped, and for once even the efficient Sulu had forgotten to call off a change in helm status.

Decker became aware that the Ilia mechanism was moving away from him and toward the turbolift elevator landing, then Kirk turned toward him with an odd, grim expression and spoke softly.

'Your opinion, Will? If I give the order to Scott now, it may surprise Vejur.'

Decker understood perfectly what Kirk meant. 'It's interest in finding the Creator could be distracting it, sir – at this moment, anyway.'

'Bridge to engineering,' called Kirk, still quietly.

'Yes, sir? I'm ready, if that's what you're wondering,' answered Sott's voice.

'Well . . .'

Kirk hesitated. Vejur was ready to take them to its very brain core! Was it possible that there could be anything to learn there that would justify the risk of waiting too long? Kirk looked up and called to the Ilia mechanism.

'Wait. I said we would disclose the information in Vejur's presence. What . . . *part* of Vejur is over there?'

'Vejur's beginning.'

Spock was on his feet, his curiosity almost cat-like. 'Fascinating, Captain. It said that almost . . . *reverently*.'

'Jim, lad . . . 'tis a terrible thing you're doing to me.' It was Scott's voice from the intercom. Kirk whirled guiltily – he had completely forgotten leaving Scott there in mid-command.

'Stand by, Mister Scott,' he said lamely. 'I think we'll just stay with the timing I gave you.'

'I've half a mind to push the damned button on you,' came Scott's reply. 'But I'll wait. Engineer out.'

The Ilia-probe had taken Kirk and the others by turbolift to a dimly lit maintenance shaft. It was obvious that Vejur knew every detail of the Enterprise as its probe then led them unerringly to a small maintenance lift and motioned them to step onto it. There was hardly room for all five of them as the inspection lift then began traveling upward – an access hatch slid aside over their heads and suddenly the lift was carrying them out in the open. It came to a stop and they found themselves standing without spacesuits on the surface of the saucer hull of the Enterprise!

Kirk heard a surprised gasp from Decker and realized that he had very nearly done the same. The sweep and symmetry of their starship was bathed in the golden glow – it looked almost impossibly lovely.

'We *are* in an atmosphere and gravity envelope, just as promised,' announced Spock. 'Fascinating.'

McCoy gave the probe a quick look, as if suspecting some trickery. Out here, their lungs should have ruptured and their frozen bodies should not be floating about weightlessly.

The Ilia-probe was already walking out toward the front edge of the saucer section. It was only as Kirk turned to follow her that he realized that Decker's gasp of astonishment had little to do with the look of Enterprise from here. Even in Kirk's eyes, the starship seemed to shrink in size as he took in the awesome reality surrounding them. A fleet of starships could have maneuvered in the vastness of Vejur's brain hemisphere, yet, according to Spock, this great hemisphere was far from being mere empty space – it was actually a great complex of electromagnetic wave-particles which carried Vejur's conscious thoughts just as the nerves and neurons in

Kirk's brain did the same for him. And Kirk's mind reeled as he realized that the sheer immensity of all this was linked also to the equally incredible storage capacity of the memory crystals described by Spock.

They were led to the edge of their ship's saucer section. Here, the Ilia mechanism stopped and stood looking out toward the brain hemisphere nucleus which they had examined earlier on the bridge viewer.

'Undoubtedly our destination,' said Spock quietly. 'We've begun to move in that direction.'

Spock was right, no doubt of it. The glittering nucleus was looming much larger. To Kirk it began to resemble more a floating jeweled island than the central part of a living brain.

'Vejur's beginning,' said the probe. It was pointing toward the nucleus.

'Vejur's *beginning*?' asked Kirk. 'What does that mean?'

The probe continued to ignore him.

'Ilia, help us. At least explain to us what's happening.' It was Decker, trying again, but the probe gave no sign of hearing him.

The brain center was much closer and the bright pillar of light at its center was more pronounced, glaring almost blindingly bright. They had come to only a dozen ship lengths away from it. Its finely detailed structural patterns were so unlike anything in Kirk's experience that he could not even guess at their function. But at least it appeared to be solid matter of some kind – they would be able to find footholds to move about on if that was indeed where the probe was taking them.

Kirk's mind raced. They were only moments away and he had no illusions but that he would be expected to provide Vejur with its Creator. He might conceivably get by with even a convincing description – certainly that had satisfied humans for enough centuries. But how could he even guess at what would satisfy Vejur?

Vejur's beginning. Think! Spock saw a machine planet. But it was located on the other side of our galaxy, far beyond the range of our starships. What could possibly make something from there believe that its Creator is here?

Kirk came out of his thoughts suddenly, realizing that something unexpected had just happened. Of course! The starship's motion had stopped, but they were a ship length or more away from the nucleus.

'Jim!' 'Captain!' Exclamations from McCoy and Decker as a pattern of tumbling shapes came rushing toward them at alarming speed. They appeared to be great translucent rectangles of light which were somehow solidifying into matter as they came. Then the shapes made a sweeping pirouette and settled in gently between them and the hemisphere's 'island' nucleus.

Kirk literally disbelieved his own eyes for a moment. The shapes had formed themselves into a floating *pathway* across to whatever awaited them over there.

The starship nudged up with a gentle bump against the pathway pattern and then the Ilia-probe stepped out onto the first floating shape. Like a glowing ice floe, it supported the probe as it stepped to another, then another. McCoy started to throw a frowning 'I refuse to do that' look, but Kirk followed the probe immediately, with Spock and Decker stepping onto a floating shape behind him. McCoy was left with no option but to follow. He was surprised and immensely relieved to find that caution was unnecessary – the glowing shapes seemed almost intelligently anxious to accommodate each footstep with perfect traction and balance.

'Ten minutes, Captain,' said Spock. The Vulcan had his tricorder out, scanning and examining with each step of the way.

Kirk had a sick feeling that they had run out of time. There was nothing that could be seen or said which could solve anything in that short a time. The gigantic machine must not have any suspicion that he had no answers about the Creator. Vejur would no more hesitate destroying carbon-based life on that planet than McCoy would hesitate over destroying cancer cells if he ever ran across them.

As they reached the complex, their eyes could pierce the light glare enough to see that its center area sloped upward from all directions like a giant inverted bowl. The slightly convex sides steepened at the top where the shining pillar of light beamed out of a wide opening. There was no doubt now where they were being led.

'This nucleus area,' said Spock, checking his tricorder, 'is older than the rest of Vejur. Although it is still well beyond our understanding, none of it appears as advanced as the rest of Vejur.'

'Which fits an idea I've been forming,' said McCoy. 'From an anatomical point of view, I would describe this as the nucleus of the hemisphere brain all around us.'

Spock was suddenly very interested. 'Are you thinking *primal* brain, Doctor?'

McCoy nodded, turning to Kirk, 'I don't know how much this will help, but I'd guess that this place here connects what Vejur is now with what Vejur used to be.'

They were climbing up a steepening incline, only a dozen steps from the brilliant light beam. They could see that the opening out of which it rose was as wide as an amphitheatre. Kirk found himself hurrying, feeling rising excitement. Great pillars surrounded it. If a machine could have conceived Stonehenge, this was such a place. Shielding their eyes from the light glare, they clambered to the edge of the opening and looked down into it – and came to a shuffling, shocked halt.

There was stunned surprise on every face, except that of the probe. It simply indicated and said: 'Vejur.'

The wide concave area below them was actually not unlike a small amphitheatre – the pillar of light somehow carried the feeling of a sacred flame, as if marking something immeasurably sacred to Vejur. That object was pitted and damage-scarred, but still undeniably *a twentieth century space probe from planet Earth*.

'I doubt that Vejur will believe the truth,' murmured Spock.

'You can be damned certain it won't,' said McCoy.

CHAPTER TWENTY-EIGHT

Kirk stepped up to the gold surfaced plaque on the old probe. Most of the inscription was still legible:

V   GER 6

NASA

Between the V and G was a torn, gaping hole, mute record of some encounter with space hazard. 'V-GER . . . *Vejur!*' said Kirk. He traced a finger where the letters had been obliterated. 'V-O-Y-A-G-E-R . . . Voyager Six!'

This particular space capsule was well known to the four Starfleet officers. Its history was studied by every Starfleet cadet, Voyager Six having been the first human-made object to enter a time continuum, although the reason for its sudden disappearance had not been understood at the time.

'I shot an arrow into the air . . .' said McCoy.

Kirk nodded, looking at the NASA symbol. What would they have thought of the way *this* arrow fell back to Earth?

'It re-entered normal space on the far side of the galaxy,' said Kirk to Spock, 'and must have wandered into the gravitational field of the planet you saw. The great machines there repaired it. . . .'

'More than that,' said Spock. 'They discovered its programming – and, being machines themselves, they obeyed.'

'*The Creator commands* . . .' nodded McCoy.

'It's twentieth-century programming would have been

very simple,' said Decker. 'Collect all possible data; transmit those findings.'

Kirk nodded. *'Learn all that is learnable; return that information to the Creator.'*

'And the machines obeyed literally,' said Spock. 'They equipped Voyager with scanning and measuring devices from their own advanced technology, and also gave it the power needed to return to Earth as commanded.'

It was difficult not to feel awed over Vejur's magnificent odyssey.

'And on the long journey back, it gathered so much knowledge that it achieved consciousness,' said Decker.

'You will now disclose the information,' demanded the Ilia-probe.

'We now have seven minutes, Jim,' said Spock quietly. Kirk gave the Vulcan a nod. Even with all this, there was something comforting in hearing Spock use his first name again.

'Well, at least *we* know what its answer is,' said McCoy. 'But if I were Vejur, I certainly wouldn't believe us.'

'Unless we can prove we're right,' said Decker, 'and I think we can! The binary code signal that Vejur sent out was part of the Voyager design – a signal meaning that it had data to transmit. And NASA was then supposed to send a signal back, instructing it to transmit that data!'

'Kirk-unit, why has the Creator not answered?' The Ilia-probe's tone was harsh.

'Captain to Enterprise,' said Kirk into his communicator.

Uhura's voice came back immediately: 'Enterprise.'

'Kirk-unit, you will supply the information *now*! Why has the Creator not . . .'

Kirk interrupted: 'The Creator will explain that itself. Vejur will have its answer in a few . . .'

'There will be no further delay. You will describe the Creator immediately!'

'Vejur! If your probe keeps interfering, the Creator will *never* answer!'

Kirk turned his back on the probe, lifting his communicator again, speaking quickly: 'We need this fast, Uhura. Order up ship's library records on late twentieth-century NASA probe, Voyager Six; specifically, get us the old NASA code signal and frequency ordering Voyager to transmit data collected.'

'Aye, sir.' From his communicator, Kirk could hear his own voice coming from the bridge speakers as Uhura relayed his actual command in the most efficient way possible.

Spock was using his tricorder to examine the way in which the base of the Voyager capsule seemed to merge into and become part of Vejur's brain nucleus design. It was also Kirk's first moment in which to glance around, and his eyes were drawn underfoot, where he could see faint light glows which indicated that the NASA capsule was still functioning and was interconnected with the great Vejur all around them.

Then Kirk's eyes were drawn to the Ilia-probe. It looked different somehow. McCoy and Decker were looking at it in astonishment, and McCoy was motioning to him.

'Vejur seems to have taken your threat literally. . . . It's released control of the probe.'

'Ilia,' said Decker, 'tell the Captain what's happened.'

'I . . . I've been here, *in* here. It was like I was dreaming it . . . and then Will was . . . helping me wake up!' The probe turned toward Decker. 'I wanted to help you, but Vejur knew it and took control of . . . of this *body* I'm in . . .'

'She's *alive*,' said Decker to Kirk. 'Somehow Vejur was able to put the *living person* in there. . . .'

'It *is* Ilia, Jim,' said McCoy. 'You can even *see* it!'

Bones was right – there was *life* in her eyes, a *living* expression on her face. Seized with a sudden idea, Kirk indicated Voyager Six. 'Ilia, do you remember this from Academy history?'

'Ilia' looked, nodded immediately. 'Yes, of course, it . . . it . . . *Misinformation is forbidden, Kirk-unit!*' It was suddenly the probe again – cold, mechanical.

'No! No, damn it . . .' shouted Decker. His voice was drowned in deafening thunder-sounds – above them, the great pillar of light seemed to explode into fragments as the brain nucleus 'island' trembled beneath their feet.

'Enterprise, come in!' called Kirk into his communicator.

Uhura was answering before he finished. 'We've just received the response code, sir.'

'Broadcast it!' interrupted Kirk. 'Now!' Then he whirled to the Ilia-probe. 'Vejur, the Creator will answer you *now*!'

Spock had come hurrying back to them from the Voyager capsule. Decker still retained enough presence of mind to take Spock's tricorder and set in the radio frequency just given by Uhura. The ominous flashes and thundering sounds began to subside. From the tricorder in Decker's hand, they could hear the thin, high-pitched code signal begin.

In the same instant, there was the faint sound of a short-circuit arc from the direction of Voyager Six.

Spock's acute hearing picked it up – he turned in time to see a faint curl of smoke briefly visible at the capsule's maintenance hatch. Meanwhile, the code signal could still be heard coming from the tricorder as Uhura completed transmitting it.

'Signal has been sent, Captain,' said Uhura's voice. 'Shall we repeat?'

'Jim, she's back,' said Decker.

'What?' Kirk could not imagine what Decker was talking about until he saw that he had taken the probe's hand. *Why in the hell was Decker doing that at a time like this?*

Kirk stepped in, confronting the probe as before: '*Vejur! The Creator has responded!*'

'Yes, sir?' said Ilia's voice.

'Captain, over here, please.' It was Spock, calling urgently from the Voyager Six capsule. He was opening the cover to the small maintenance hatch there.

The Vulcan stepped aside, indicating into the hatch. 'You will notice, Captain, that the transceiver antenna connection has been burned through.'

Kirk looked inside – a small, dark burn mark could be seen where the wiring had parted. He made the mistake of reaching in to explore it with his finger . . . and yanked his hand back in surprise.

'What the hell?! It's still hot!'

'Exactly, Captain. Vejur did that just as the signal began.'

'It *can't* have done that, Spock! Vejur is *desperate* to hear from its Creator!'

'It is desperate to *unite* with its Creator, Captain. The probe told us that, but we did not understand.'

McCoy nodded. '*Vejur's purpose is to survive . . . to unite with the Creator.* But I thought the probe meant that metaphorically. . . .'

'Vejur speaks and interprets *everything* literally,' said Spock as he looked around at the amphitheatre design. 'It no doubt plans to unite physically with the Creator here.'

'Do you mean what I think you're saying Spock?' asked McCoy. '*Vejur is planning to capture God?*'

'It is the perfectly logical thing for Vejur to do,' said Spock. 'Vejur knows itself to be incomplete, but has no way of learning what it needs . . . or whether the Creator would even agree to provide it.' Spock pointed to the severed antenna connection. 'Ergo! For the Creator to obtain Vejur's knowledge, it must bring the signal here in person.'

It was a stunning revelation. Kirk realized that Spock must be right; it was the most certain answer that Vejur could have. By its very nature, a Creator *has* and *is* every answer to everything.

'Where is Decker?' Kirk was realizing the exec and the Ilia mechanism had been missing through most of this. McCoy indicated past Voyager Six where the two were talking together quietly, hands joined. Kirk did not have the heart to summon him – even if the rest of them somehow survived, there was no way to know what would happen to Ilia's living consciousness.

'We now have four minutes,' said Spock.

'*Three*,' corrected Kirk. 'I ordered Scott to go two-zero-zero-five a minute earlier.'

'Well?' asked McCoy. 'We can't very well deliver the people who actually built Voyager . . .'

'Spock, we need an answer,' said Kirk. 'Will it accept *us*?'

218

Spock was eyeing the twentieth-century capsule and the nucleus design around it. 'As Doctor McCoy said, we all create God in our image. Vejur still expects a machine . . . it probably plans something similar to what occurs in our ship's transporter chamber, except that *two* forms will be reduced to energy . . .'

'. . . and combined both of them together into a new form.' It was Decker's voice – he and Ilia were standing at this side of the Voyager capsule now, with Spock's tricorder still in Decker's hand.

'Request permission to proceed, Captain.' Decker was making an adjustment on the tricorder.

'Wait,' said Kirk. 'We'll discuss *who* does it only after we're certain of what . . .'

'Jim, it's got to be done – with or without your permission.'

As Decker's eyes turned to the open access hatch, Kirk moved in, grabbing for the exec's arm, but the Ilia mechanism lifted Kirk away as though he were a child, sending him sprawling at Spock and McCoy's feet. As he started to his feet again, he felt a hand restraining him.

'Let it happen, Captain,' said Spock's voice. 'I suspect he knows exactly what he's doing.'

Decker nodded. 'I *do* know.' From the tricorder in his hand they could hear the high, thin sound of the code signal beginning – a pulsating light glow was appearing all around the base of Voyager Six.

'I want this!' called Decker. 'Just as you wanted the Enterprise.' At the same time, Decker placed the tricorder into the Voyager's open hatch, pushing it into contact with the space capsule's transceiver.

Something was happening to the great pillar of white light thrusting up around them. It was . . . *trembling* like a live thing – a lovely thing in which spiraling brilliant colors began to appear – the colors began fanning out over their heads like great unfolding blossoms.

Even Spock's eyes were widening – there was breathtaking *beauty* in what was happening. It was becoming all beauty, driving out any feeling of fear they might have had. McCoy was standing transfixed. Kirk became aware that they were also *hearing* beauty – and *feeling* it, too.

At the center of the cascading colors, Decker's body was beginning to glow with the same brilliance and there was a look of serenity on his face – the same look was on Ilia's face as she stepped into the spiraling colors with him.

'Jim . . . this is *transcendence*!' It was Spock, indicating around them where the entire concave amphitheatre was beginning to glow – the brain nucleus material under their feet becoming transparent and deep down inside it they could see a great whorl of spiraling color that was growing in size and brightness like some immense flower blossoming into life.

The doctor had almost a look of rapture on his face and Kirk had to shake him to get his attention. 'We've got to get back to the ship.'

The forms of Decker and Ilia were still *expanding*, perfect serenity on both their faces as the spiraling colors became part of them – and their gigantic shapes began becoming part of Vejur.

The three officers turned and hurried up the concave of the amphitheatre design. As they hurried over the top lip of it, they could see the entire brain nucleus 'island' was aglow. They headed for Enterprise on a run – even the great brain hemisphere around them was shimmering into lovely patterns. Vejur was transcending – flowering – taking new form.

They ran out of air, or would have by human standards – Spock's Vulcan lungs held out longest and he virtually carried them onto the starship's saucer section, where spacesuited figures hurried them through the hatch and into the airlock.

On the bridge, they had a last look at the *transcendence*. *It then became too lovely for them to comprehend, and so it was gone without ever really leaving.*

When Kirk began to relate to the here and the now of the Enterprise bridge, he turned to Spock. 'I wonder, did we just see the beginning of a new form of life out there?'

'Yes, Captain. We witnessed a birth – perhaps also a direction in which some of us may evolve.'

'Only *some* of us, Spock?'

'It would seem to me, Captain, that the dimensions of creation make our future choices almost limitless.'

'It's been a long time since I helped deliver a baby,' said McCoy. 'I hope we humans gave this one a good start.'

'I think we did,' Kirk answered. 'The Decker part of us gives it the ability to want and to enjoy, to hope and to dare and pretend and laugh.' Kirk smiled at his next thought. 'And the child will probably have some very interesting Deltan attributes, too. It should have an exciting future.'

McCoy gave a look toward Spock. 'And our other emotions? Fear, greed, jealousy, hate . . .?'

'Those things are the *mis-use* of emotion, Doctor,' said Spock.

Kirk found himself feeling very comfortable as he

settled himself back into the center seat. He was realizing that there was a certain shrewd and sometimes ruthless commanding admiral down there, who right now would be unable to deny him anything – even permanent command of the Enterprise if Kirk demanded it. Well, that suited former Admiral James Tiberius Kirk fine. He did not intend to let Heihachiro Nogura get off this hook.

'Interrogative from Starfleet,' Uhura said. 'They request damage and injury report and complete vessel status.'

'Vessel status operational. List Security Officer Phillips, Lieutenant Ilia, and Captain Decker . . . list them as *missing*.'

'Aye, sir, and Starfleet also requests that you and your department heads beam down immediately for debriefing.'

'Answer . . . request denied.'

'Sir?' Uhura was looking toward him, startled.

'Simply answer *request denied*. Isn't that clear enough, Commander?'

Uhura understood, and she smiled: 'Aye, sir. It should be clear to one and all.'

Kirk turned to see Chief Engineer Scott coming onto the bridge with Doctor Chapel. 'Scotty, isn't it about time we gave the Enterprise a proper shakedown?'

Scott was instantly pleased. 'I would say it's time for that, sir. *Aye!*' He turned to Spock. 'We can have you back on Vulcan in four days, Mister Spock.'

'Unnecessary, Mister Scott. My task on Vulcan is completed.'

Kirk turned to the helm. 'Take us out of orbit, Mister Sulu.'

'Heading, sir?' DiFalco asked.

Kirk indicated generally ahead. 'Out there. Thataway.'

'A most logical choice, Captain,' Spock said.

The main viewer switched to show the lovely blue-white sphere receding behind them. As Kirk watched it grow still smaller, he decided that Earth was a place that he would never want to live without – and yet he would not want to live there permanently, either. At least, not for a very long time.

'Viewer ahead, go to warp one.'

'Accelerating to warp one, sir,' said Sulu.

At first, there were the old familiar star patterns. And then the quantum shift happened; the star mass congealed in front of them and they were in hyperspace. He relaxed back and began thinking about where he would take her first.

All Futura Books are available at your bookshop or
newsagent, or can be ordered from the following
address:
Futura Books, Cash Sales Department,
P.O. Box 11, Falmouth, Cornwall.

Please send cheque or postal order (no currency), and
allow 25p for postage and packing for the first book
plus 10p per copy for each additional book ordered up to
a maximum charge of £1.05 in U.K.

Customers in Eire and B.F.P.O. please allow 25p for
postage and packing for the first book plus 10p per copy
for the next eight books, thereafter 5p per book.

Overseas customers please allow 40p for postage and
packing for the first book and 12p per copy for each
additional book.